PENGUIN BOOKS

MAGGIE CASSIDY

Jack Kerouac was born in Lowell, Massachusetts, in 1922, the youngest of three children in a Franco-American family. He attended local Catholic and public schools and won a football scholarship to Columbia University in New York City, where he met Neal Cassady, Allen Ginsberg, and William S. Burroughs. He quit school in his sophomore year after a dispute with his football coach and joined the Merchant Marine, beginning the restless wanderings that were to continue for the greater part of his life. His first novel, *The Town and the City,* appeared in 1950, but it was *On the Road,* first published in 1957 and memorializing his adventures with Neal Cassady, that epitomized to the world what became known as "the Beat generation" and made Kerouac one of the most controversial and best-known writers of his time. Publication of his many other books followed, among them *The Dharma Bums, The Subterraneans,* and *Big Sur.* Kerouac considered them all to be part of *The Duluoz Legend.* "In my old age," he wrote, "I intend to collect all my work and reinsert my pantheon of uniform names, leave the long shelf full of books there, and die happy." He died in St. Petersburg, Florida, in 1969, at the age of forty-seven.

BY JACK KEROUAC

THE TOWN AND THE CITY

THE SCRIPTURE OF THE GOLDEN ETERNITY

SOME OF THE DHARMA

OLD ANGEL MIDNIGHT

GOOD BLONDE AND OTHERS

PULL MY DAISY

TRIP TRAP

PIC

THE PORTABLE JACK KEROUAC

SELECTED LETTERS: 1940–1956

POETRY

MEXICO CITY BLUES

SCATTERED POEMS

POMES ALL SIZES

HEAVEN AND OTHER POEMS

BOOK OF BLUES

THE DULUOZ LEGEND

VISIONS OF GERARD

DOCTOR SAX

MAGGIE CASSIDY

VANITY OF DULUOZ

ON THE ROAD

VISIONS OF CODY

THE SUBTERRANEANS

TRISTESSA

LONESOME TRAVELLER

DESOLATION ANGELS

THE DHARMA BUMS

BOOK OF DREAMS

BIG SUR

SATORI IN PARIS

Maggie Cassidy

Jack Kerouac

PENGUIN BOOKS

PENGUIN BOOKS
Published by the Penguin Group
Penguin Books USA Inc., 375 Hudson Street, New York,
New York 10014, U.S.A.
Penguin Books Ltd, 27 Wrights Lane, London W8 5TZ, England
Penguin Books Australia Ltd, Ringwood, Victoria, Australia
Penguin Books Canada Ltd, 10 Alcorn Avenue, Toronto,
Ontario, Canada M4V 3B2
Penguin Books (N.Z.) Ltd, 182–190 Wairau Road,
Auckland 10, New Zealand

Penguin Books Ltd, Registered Offices:
Harmondsworth, Middlesex, England

First published in the United States of America by
Avon Books, 1959
Published in Penguin Books 1993

20 19 18 17 16 15 14 13 12

The lyrics appearing on pages 26 & 27 are from *Deep in a Dream*,
copyright © Harms, Inc., 1938. Used by permission.

LIBRARY OF CONGRESS CATALOGING IN PUBLICATION DATA
Kerouac, John, 1922–1969.
Maggie Cassidy.
I. Title.
ISBN 0 14 01.7906 2
PZ3.K4596Mag 1978 PS3521.E735
813′.5′4   77–25167

Printed in the United States of America

Maggie Cassidy

1

It was a New Year's Eve, it was snowing in the North. The fellows were staggering down the snowy road arm in arm supporting a central figure who all alone was singing in a cracked sad broken voice what he had heard the cowboy sing in the Gates Theater Friday afternoon, *"Jack o diamonds, Jack o diamonds, you'll be my downfall,"* but not knowing the downfall part of it, just *Jack o* where it broke and yodeled in a western-type twang. This was G.J. Rigopoulos singing. His head hung low like a drunk's as they dragged his shoes through the snow, arms limp and hips hanging out like an idiot's in a tremendous display of complete didnt care attitude that had all the others struggling and slipping in the snow to hold him up. But from his brokendoll neck came the plaintive notes, *Jack o diamonds, Jack o diamonds*, as great thick snowflakes dropped straight on their heads. It was the New Year 1939, before the war, before anyone knew the intention of the world toward America.

The boys were all French Canadian except the Greek lad G.J. It had never occurred to any of them, the others, Scotty Boldieu, Albert Lauzon, Vinny Bergerac and Jacky Duluoz, to wonder that G.J. had spent his entire boyhood with them instead of with other Greek boys for close companions and soulmates of puberty, when all he had to do was walk across the river and see a thousand Greek boys or go up the Paw-tucketville hill to a fair-sized Greek neighborhood and find many friends. It might have occurred to Lauzon that G.J.

never ended among the Greeks, to Lousy who was the most sympathetic and thoughtful of the gang; but since everything occurred to him, he never mentioned any part of it—yet. But the love that went out from all four French boys to this Greek boy was fantastic, true-volumed, bleakfaced and innocent of other things in the world and completely serious. They hung on him for dear life, twitching to see each new joke he might choose next in his role as King's Comedian. They were walking under immense beautiful dark-limbed trees of black winter, dark arms twisted and sinuous from sidewalk up; they overtopped the road, Riverside Street, in a solid roof for several blocks past phantasmal old homes with huge porches and Christmas lights buried deep in; real-estate relics of when to be on the river meant and called for expensive building. But now Riverside Street was a hodge-podge running from a tiny brownly lit Greek variety store at the edge of a sand field, with riverward bungalow streets going down; from it to a sandlot baseball field more or less the scene of overgrown weeds, foulballs breaking windows, and October night fires of hoodlums and urchins of the town, to which category G.J. and his gang had, and still belonged.

"Give me a snowball, men," said G.J. snapping out of his drunken act, staggering; Lauzon leaping to the issue handing him the snowball with an expectant giggle.

"What you gonna do, Mouse?"

"Gonna belt that poor poss bowling around!" he snarled. "Make revolutions swim around! Burpers'll raise big legs to poop on southern shores, Palm Miami Beach—" and he threw his snowball with a vicious long whip of his arm at a passing car and popped right in the front a soft plopping exploding snowball that left a star shining in the glass and in their eyes as they all heaved to laugh and throw themselves slapping on their knees, the pop had been just loud enough to attract the attention of the motorist, who was driving an old loud-motored Essex with a load of wood in the back and a Christmas tree and a few logs and a few more in front with a little kid holding up against them, his son, farmers from Dracut; he just turned and glowered briefly and drove on grimly toward Mill Pond and the pines of old tar roads.

"Ha ha ha did you see the expression on his face?" yelled Vinny Bergerac with shuddering eagerness jumping up around the road and grabbing G.J. to haul and push him in a wild laughing hysterical stagger of joy. They were almost falling in a snowbank.

A little to the side, and quiet, walked Scotty Boldieu, head bent in thought as if he were studying a cigarette's tip alone in a room; bulky-shouldered, short, hawkfaced and sleek, a little dark, brown-eyed. He turned to throw a little inward-thinking and courteous laugh with the others in their general uproar. At the same time in his eyes there was a twinkle of disbelief in their antics at his somber side, grave and surprised recognition of them, a kind of leadership of the silent sailing soul in all of them, so Lousy seeing him thus interior-bemused away from the hilarity leaned his head on his shoulder a second in an old sister's laugh and shook him to see: "Hey Scotty didnt you see El Mouso hurl that apple right on the guy's window, just like when he threw his ice cream at the screen in the movie about the foreclose mortgage at the Crown? Cheez! What a maniac! Zeet?"

Scotty just waved his hand and nodded, biting his lip, and took a deep brooding drag on a Chesterfield cigarette,

probably his thirtieth or fortieth of a new lifetime, seventeen
years old and bound to sink down to his work in slow,
heavy, relaxed degrees, tragic and beautiful to see the snow
bedeck his eyebrows and hatless well-combed head.

Vinny Bergerac was as skinny as a stick, screaming all
the time, happy; his father's name must have been Joy;
inside his crazy-flapping coat of activities and yells with the
gang his little thin, wasted body swiveled on inexistent hips
and long, white, tragic legs. His face was thin as a razor,
sharply handsome, cut with a fingernail file; blue eyes, white
teeth, shining, mad eyes; his hair was wet, combed forward
to a roll, slicked back with a brush, smooth and dark under
his white silk scarf; his eyebrows stood out somewhat like
Tyrone Power eyebrows of conscious perfect good looks. But
he was a scatterbrained madman from the word go. His
laugh crashed and shrieked all over the silent snowy road
of huddled holiday workers bending to their work with
bottles and packages, noses sniffling in the night. Snow
dropped on his head and through the wild streams of his
cries. G.J. had risen from his grave of snow, where "That
ga-dam rat" he'd fallen, it being soft he sank shudderingly
in the cold; now, coming up white, he had Vinny under
the belt on his shoulder giving him the whirlaround airplane
throw they'd all seen in wrestling matches at the Rex and
the CMAC and in their own backyards promoted by themselves—wild, yelling, they danced around the inevitable
climax in proud flapping topcoats of adolescence.

They hadn't even begun to drink.

G.J. and Vinny collapsed together in the snowbank, sank,
everybody danced and howled; the snow flew, some fell from
shivered branches in the high night; it was New Year's Eve.

2

Albert Lauzon turned his sad eyes on Jack Duluoz, who was unexpectedly pensive beside him.

"Hey Zaaaagg didja see him? Mouse giving him the old flying wedge tackle—what do you call that hold Zagg? Zeet?" This was a convulsive little fizzle giggle in his teeth. "That crazy Vinny had him down did you see that sneaky rat sink him in five miles deep in the zeet? Hey Zagg?" and grasping Zagg by the arm to shake him and make him see what had just happened. But some distant hung-up recollection or reflection had taken hold of the other boy's mind and he had to turn around and look carefully at Lousy to understand what reaction was expected of him at that moment when he had been dreaming. Lauzon's sad eyes he saw, set somewhat close on each side of a long strange nose, something shrouded and hidden beneath a large brown felt hat, the only one in the gang wearing a hat; and revealing nothing but an expectant laugh blazing wildly with youth in the closeup eyes, the long jaw, long mouth drawn to wait and see him. A twinge, a flicker of something, barely touched the corner of Lauzon's mouth as he saw Zagg's long hesitation returning from his own thoughts; some disappointment had come and gone forever in his study of the other boy; and in his own mind Zagg Duluoz had only been thinking of the time when he was four years old and in the red May late afternoon he had thrown a rock at a car in front of the firehouse and the car stopped and the man got out with a great worried expression and the glass was broken, so seeing the flick of disappointment in Lauzon he wondered

9

if he should tell him about the rock of four years old but Lauzon was ahead of him. "Zagg you missed seeing the great Mouse being downed by skinny boy Vinny Bergerac it's sensational!" And Lauzon was giving him hell. "No kidding you was off a million miles then, you didn't see, it'll never be forgotten: imagine the one and only G.J.—look what he's doing now! Zagg you crazy! Zeet!" slapping him and pulling him and shaking him. It was all forgotten in a second. The perturbation bird had flown in, and sat on pearly souls, and gone again. At the edge of the gang trudged Scotty, still alone, still inside.

G.J. nicknamed Mouse and born Rigopoulos, or probably Rigolopoulakos and shortened by his hard-working parents, was now up and unjokingly or trying seriously if possible gravely to brush the snow off his new coat thinking just then of his mother who'd so proudly given it to him last week Christmas. "Easy boys, lay off, my old lady just gave me this cashmere coat here, the price tag was so abnormable I had to put my own immemoriam sign——" but suddenly his vigor and vitality leaped out of him again with the force of an explosion, his interest in everybody was so absolutely boundless it was like a compulsive drunk's leap to rush, to begin anew, exhaust the world, kiss the foundations of the world——"Zagg hey Zagg hey! what's that immemorious word you told me on the Square not on the Square right in front the City Hall the other night, you said you read it in the encyclopediac, Zagg, the word with the monument——

"—immemor—"

"Immemorialamums— Hayee!" screamed Mouse leaping at Zagg across the arms of the gang and grabbing him with a feverish anxiety. "The immemorials of the world war

monuments—six million memorials of the—Wadworth
Longfellow—long far—Zagg what is that word? Tell us
what . . . that . . . word . . . is!" he yelled with great ur-
gency pulling and pulling at him to show him to the others,
with a frantic act of being so excited and so "blafferfasted"
as he said that at any moment he would fly into the air from
inpent unkeepable explosions of suspense. It was, in his
charade, a matter of such great importance that to say the
least—"This man must be beheaded at once, call the Tower,
twelve sixty-nine, calling the lines in the desk, calling the
moon, we got him on our blockheads ready to go, this man
refuses to tell us, Boris Karloff and company and Bela Loo-
boosi and us vampires and everybody connected with Fran-
kenstein and . . ." with a sly whisper—"the . . . house . . .
of . . . Muxy Smith . . ." At which everybody reared back
exploding with laughter and amazement; only a few weeks
ago they had carried an old drunk of Pawtucketville home
to his house far down Riverside Street, and it happened to
be a 175-year-old unpainted Colonial house crumbling from
hearth to doorstone in its sad sunken field just off a fork
of roads to Dracut and Lakeview; it was spooky, night; they
stumbled the little old man into his kitchen, he flopped,
mumbled; said he heard ghosts all the time in the other
rooms; as they were leaving the old man stumbled on a
rocking chair and fell and hit his head and lay on the floor
moaning. They helped him dragfooted to a couch; he seemed
to be all right. But they heard the wind in the eaves, the
unused attic upstairs . . . they all hurried home. And the
nearer they got home the more G.J., talking excitedly even
then, became convinced Muxy Smith was dead, had killed
himself. "He's on that couch pale as a sheet and dead as a

ghost," whispered, "I'm telling you . . . from now on it's
going to be the ghost of Muxy Smith"; and so that in the
morning, a Sunday, they had all looked with apprehension
at the newspaper to read and see if Muxy Smith had been
found dead in his haunted old house. "I knew that moon
was out when we met him on that Textile sidewalk—bad
sign, we should never taken him home the old guy is half
dead," G.J. kept saying at midnight. But in the morning
no news to the effect that a bunch of boys had slipped away
from a house, leaving a dead man bruised with a heavy
object; so they visited each other after church, the French
Canadians going to Sainte Jeanne d'Arc on the Pawtucketville hill, and G.J. across the river with his dark-veiled
mother and sisters to the Byzantine Greek Orthodox church
near the canal, and were reassured. "Muxy Smith," G.J.
whispered in the New Year's Eve snow, "and his immemoriam jazz band is coming on the sheets up there. . . . But
what a word! Hey Lousy didja hear that word? Scot? IM-
MEMORIAM. Forever and ever in stone. That's what it
means. Only Zagg could have discovered such a word. Years
he studied in his room, learning . . . IMMEMORIAM. Zagg,
Memory Babe, write some more words like that. You'll be
great. They'll make you honorary chairman of the burper's
convention of general farts in the motors division of the
superintendents of Wall Street. I'll be there, Zagg, with
a beautiful blonde, a flask, an apartment waiting for your
convenience . . . ah gentlemen I'm tired. It was a wrestling
match that—how can I dance tonight? How can I go and
jitterbug now?" And once again, everything else exhausted
for the while, he sang *Jack o diamonds* in that way he'd just
learned, sad, incredibly sad like a dog act, or like men

singing, floating broken and prophetic in the snow of the
night, *Jack o diamonds*, as arm in arm they all scuffled to
the New Year's Eve dance at the Rex Ballroom, their first
dance each one, their first and last future before them.

3

Meanwhile all this time across the street walking parallel
with them was Zaza Vauriselle who but for a prognathic
big almost hydrocephalic's jaw and six inches less height
could have been Vinny Bergerac's chiseled French Canadian
happy smiling brother; he was with the group but for awhile
had absented himself to the other sidewalk in the way of
one accustomed to walking long distances with gangs, to
think, to drive his legs on in a thing of his own, every now
and then, too, saying to them, barely heard, comments like
"Damn bunch of fools" (in French, *gange de baza*) or, "Aw
look the nice girls coming out that house hey."

Zaza Vauriselle was the oldest in the gang, had only
recently injected himself via Vinny's invitation, and had
made a hit with the rest skeptical or not only because he
was such a fantastic fool, capable of any joke, the main joke
being, "He'll do anything Vinny says, anything"; and his
added value that he knew all about girls and sex from direct
experience. He had the same happy thin features, and handsome like Vinny, but was very short, bowlegged, funny to
look at, shifty-eyed, heavy-jawed and snorting through a
defective nose; always masturbating in front of the others,
about eighteen; yet something curiously innocent and foolish

almost angelic though admittedly silly and probably mentally retarded as he was. He too wore a white silk scarf, a
dark topcoat, rubbers, no hat, and walked purposefully
through the two-inch snow to the dance which had been
his idea; somewhere down Lakeview Avenue, in some
Centreville house where a party of adults was starting, the
boys had gone, from G.J.'s house and Zagg's house the final
meeting place, to fetch Zaza. It made for walking and rosy-
faced excitement holiday-proper; nobody had a car till that
summer. *"On va y'allez* let's go!" Zaza had yelled. Now Zaza
Vauriselle made a snowball and threw it at Vinny his champion. "Ey, Vinny, go sit on the ga-dam bowl and shut up
before I tear your legs off . . ." Softly, from across the street,
with a stupid smile that the others all fondly saw gleaming.
G.J. staggered to hear it, whispering, pointing, shushing,
"Listen what's he thinking? . . . Ga-dam Zazay!" and ran
across the street and dove on Zaza's shoulders and drove him
into a snowbank as Zaza, unused to rough treatment, yelled
in genuine anxiety "Ey! Ey!" and all sartorial in his coat
and scarf was swashed in snow; the others rushing up to
wrestle him in every direction, and finally they lifted him
to their shoulders horizontal and went on down Riverside
yelling and bearing their Zaza.

By now they had reached a deep slope of grass behind
a wooden fence, near a near-castle made of stone, with
towers, that sat high over Riverside Street. Up the grassy
slope, white in the night, began a stone wall built up and
in against a cliff, with dry pendant remnant vines now
hanging in the snow, gleaming ice; up on top of the cliff,
three houses. The middle one was G.J.'s. They were just
regular old French Canadian two-story wooden tenements,

with washlines, porches, long boards, like Frisco tenements
enduring in the fog of the North, with brown lights in the
kitchens, dim shadows, a vague sight of a religious calendar
or an overcoat on a closet door, something sad and homely
and useful and to the boys who knew nothing else the abode
of very life. G.J.'s house sat, soared, looked over gigantic
treetops of Riverside to the city a mile across the river; in
his kitchen in blowing wild storms that would obscure vistas
and clank the trees to hit the windows, Jack Frost cracking,
raging to come in the door beneath the crack as old overshoes
gleamed cold and wet in scuffly slush-halls, as people tried
to stop a draft with a folded strip of newspaper . . . in great
stormy days when there was no school, and no occasion like
New Year's Eve, G.J. with his long legs strode his mother's
linoleum swearing and cursing the day he was born as she
an old Greek widow the death of whose husband fifteen
years ago left her still in blackest mourning, sat in a rocking
chair by the shivering window, with an old Greek bible on
her lap, and grieved, and grieved, and grieved. . . . The
sight of this house as G.J. rushed with the boys to joys
tearing in his brain . . . "Is my mother up?" he wondered—
Sometimes she just made long pitiful-to-hear lamentations
about the darkness of her life, singing it, as the children
heard every word and hung their heads in shame and
misery. . . . "Is Reno still home? . . . is *she* gonna take her
to that ga-dam woman for that visit. . . . Oh Lord in Heaven
above sometimes I think I was born to worry for that unhappy
old mother of mine till the day my boots sink in the ground
and there wont be no damn saver to pull *me* out—the last
of the Rigopoulakos, *elas spiti* Rigopoulakos . . . *ka, re,*"
he cursed and wrung inside his brain in Greek, squeezing

his thighs inside his coat till they burned, taking his hands out of his pockets to spread fingers at the others, bringing his tongue out eloquently to clack his teeth, saying "Thou, thou, thou . . . you cant know!" He felt like howling across the snow and over the twenty-foot stone wall high to his house with its dark and tragic windows except for one brown light in the kitchen that said nothing, showed nothing but death, and but indicated that as ever his mother had begun her vigil with an oil lamp, now in the chair later on the little couch by the stove in the kitchen with a pitiful flimsy bedcover when all the time she had a whole bed in her own room. . . . "So dark that room," grieved G.J., Gus, *Yanni* to his mother, *Yanni* sometimes when she chose to call him by his middle name and everybody in the neighborhood could hear her at sad red dusk calling him to pork-chop supper "Yanni . . . Yanni . . ." A Jack o Diamonds of other broken hearts. And Gus turned to his greatest and deepest friend whom he had named Zagg.

"Jack," taking his arm, holding the gang up, "do you see that light burning in my mother's kitchen window?"

"—I know, Gus—"

"—showing where an old woman this night as all nights when this poor blooder and fubbler tries to go out Zagg and get himself just a little bit of fun in the world"—his eyes tearing—"and not asking so much as that God, in his mercy, munifisessence, whatyoucallit Zagg, should only say 'Gus, Gus, poor Gus, pray to the angels and to me and I shall see Gus that your poor old mother—' "

"—Ah Brigash cass mi gass!" cried Zaza Vauriselle, suddenly weirdly apt so much so that Lauzon laughed his high wild giggle and everybody heard but paid no attention because listening to Gus make a real serious speech about his troubles.

"—that only for a moment my soul and heart could rest to see that my mother—Jack she's just an old woman—your father isnt dead, you dont know what it is to have an old widowed mother who has no old man like your old man Aooway Burp Emil Duluoz come in the house and lift his leg and lay a browsh, it's comforting, it makes the woman— it makes the child, me, realize, 'I got an old man, he comes in from work, he's an ugly old maniac nobody's gonna give ten cents for' Zagg but here I am—just two sisters, my brother dead, my oldest sister's married—you know, *Marie*—she used to be my mother's best . . . comforter— when Marie was around I didnt worry like I do now—Oh hell I dont—parade my trouble in front of you guys? Make you realize that my heart is broken . . . that as long as I live I'll have chains dragging me down to the oceans of sad tears that my feet are wet in already at the thought of my poor old mother in her ga-dam old black dress Zagg that— she waits for me! always waiting for me!" A commotion in the gang. "Ask Zagg! Three o'clock in the morning, we come home, we been shootin the bull maybe at Blezan's or saw Lucky on the street and exchanged a few greetings" (in his explanations waving a hand he was eager, thick-tongued, eloquent, his almost-olive skin and greenish-yellow eyes and earnest intensity like something in an ancient bazaar or court)—"and here we come, nothing's happened, but, and it's not too late, but, and there's my Ma— There's my Ma in the window with that light, waiting—asleep. I come in the kitchen I try to sneak, not wake her. She wakes up. 'Yanni?' she cries in a little voice like crying. . . . 'Ya

Ma, Yanni—I been out with Jacky Duluoz.'—'Yanni why
do you come home so late and worry me to death?' 'But Ma
it's late I know but I told you I'd be all right wouldnt go
no further than Destouches' ga-dam candy store,' and I start
to get mad and yell at her at three o'clock in the morning
and she says nothing just satisfied I'm safe and without a
sound there she goes in her dark bedroom and goes to sleep
and's up at the cracka ga-dam dawn to make my oatmeal
for school. You guys wonder I'm known as the crazy Mouse,"
he concluded seriously.

Jack Duluoz put his arm around him and then withdrew
it quickly. He tried to smile. Gus was looking at him for
confirmation of all his sorrows. "You're still the greatest
right fielder in history," said Jack.

"And the greatest relief pitcher, Mouso. You ever seen
his windup you'd die, zeet?" Lauzon coming to him and
taking his arm as they all took up the walk again.

"Oh," said Gus, "it's all a big . . . topcoat sale. You
cant read it all. Fuggit! I say, I say to you gentlemen,
fuggit—I aint never gonna say another word but reach for
my oteens of champagne silver biddles, what do you call—
big huge decanters of whisky and brew—slup—slip—the
whole world is gonna go down my hole before G.J. Rigopoulos says quits!"

They all cheered wildly; and reached the big intersection
of Pawtucketville, the corner of Riverside and Moody, swirling with excited snow across the arc lamp and on the yellow
bus and all the people shouting hellos from sidewalk to
sidewalk.

4

Down Riverside and to the right Scotty Boldieu lived with his own mother, in a wooden tenement, third floor, you went up there via some outside wooden steps that had the quality of steps in dreams as they rose from ten-foot bushes a jungle of them in the field below and took you swaying up the ladder of flimsy porches with strange-faced French Canadian ladies looking down yelling to other ladies "Aayoo Madame Belanger *a tu ton* wash finished?" Scotty had a room to himself where he spent many hours studiously writing down the summer baseball team averages in red ink in infinitestimal figures and small letters; or just sat in the brown kitchen with the *Sun* and read the sports page. There was a little brother. There was a dead father there too. It had been some big-fisted man with a grim countenance, whose trudgings to work in the morning were like the departure of the Golem across the fogs and seas of his duty. Scotty, G.J., Zagg, Lauzon, Vinny all played an important part in a summer baseball team, a winter basketball team, and an invincible autumn football team.

Lauzon lived back down Riverside Street in the direction they were coming from, down the hill from the Greek candy store at the edge of the sandbank's desert of sand, on a rosy street, among bungalows. Tall strange Lauzon's father was a tall strange milkman. His tall strange kid brother prayed and made novenas at the church with all the other kids his age doing their Confirmation. At Christmas the Lauzons had a Christmas tree, and gifts; G.J. Rigopoulos had a tree too but something sick, scraggly, forever defeated shone

from it in his dark window; Scotty Boldieu's mother put
up a tree in a linoleumed parlor with the gravity of an
undertaker, by vases. In the big Zara house trees, gifts,
window wreaths, confetti . . . his being a typical large
French Canadian home.

Vinny Bergerac lived across the river, on Moody Street,
in the slums. Jacky Zagg Duluoz lived just a stone's throw
from the intersection where they had now stopped. The
intersection had a traffic light, it illuminated the snow rosy
red, wreathy green. Wooden tenements on both corners had
most of their windows shining with red and blue lights; an
air of festivity puffed out of their chimneys; people were
below in the tar courts talking echoey chatters under clothes-
lines in the snowfall.

Jacky Duluoz's home was in a tenement several doorways
up, on another corner, where the Pawtucketville center-store
area seemed always to buzz the most, right at the lunchcart,
across the street from the bowling alley, poolhall, at the
bus stop, near the big meat market, with an empty lot on
both sides of the street where kids played their gray games
in brown weeds of winter dusk when the moon is just starting
to show with a refined, distant, unseen paleness as if it had
been frozen and also smeared with slate. He lived with his
mother, father and sister; had a room of his own, with the
fourth-floor windows staring on seas of rooftops and the
glitter of winter nights when home lights brownly wave
beneath the neater whiter blaze of stars—those stars that
in the North, in the clear nights, all hang frozen tears by
the billions, with January Milky Ways like silver taffy, veils
of frost in the stillness, huge blinked, throbbing to the slow
beat of time and universal blood. In the Duluoz home the

kitchen window looked down on bright wild street scenes; inside, the bright light showed much food, cheer, apples and oranges in bowls on white tablecloths, clean ironing boards leaned behind varnished doors, cupboards, little plates of popcorn left over from last night. In the gray afternoons Jacky Duluoz rushed home, sweating in November and December, to sit in the gloom at the kitchen table, devouring, over a chess book, whole boxes of Ritz crackers with peanut butter smeared. In the evening his big father Emil came home and sat in the dark by the radio, coughing. Through the kitchen door in the hall he rushed down pell-mell to find his friends, using the front stairs down the front rooms of the tenement only with parents and company and for sadder more formal runs— The back stairs were so dim, dusty, strange, as if loose-plastered, some day he would remember them in rueful dreams of rust and loss . . . dreams when G.J.'s shadow would fall across a piece of broken leg like pottery in the street, like modern paintings in their keen screaming lostness. . . . No idea in 1939 that the world would turn mad.

On the intersection itself a surprising number of people were passing throwing remarks across the snow. Billy Artaud was striding by at his tremendous pace, short, long-legged, arms swinging, bright teeth shining; he was the second baseman on the team; in the past few months had matured suddenly and was already rushing off to see his steady girl for the New Year's parties in downtown movies.

"There's Billy Artaud! Hooray for the Dracut Tigers!" yelled Vinny but Billy flowed right along, he was late, he saw them.

"Ah you guys whattaya doin?—here it is almost ten

o'clock and you're still fiddlin and faddlin down the road when you gonna grow up, me I've got a girl so long you suckers"—Billy Artaud was known also as "Whattaguy"—"Whattaguy with snow all over his coat that Gus Rigopoulos!" he cried, waving his hand contemptuously. "Throw him to the hot night bird!" he cried, disappearing down the long street alongside Textile Institute and fields of snow to Moody Street Bridge and the downtown lights of town, toward which a lot of other people walked and many cars rolled with their chains crunching softly, their red taillights making beautiful Christmas glows in the snow.

"And here comes Iddyboy!" they all yelled with glee as out of the gloom appeared the great figure of Joe Bissonnette who the moment he saw them turned his shoulders into huge bulking phantoms around his sunken and outthrust chin and came forward on padding cat feet. "Here comes the big Marine!"

"OO!" greeted Joe, still holding himself rigidly inside his "Marine" pose, copied off the hulks and bulks of big sea dogs in Charles Bickford films of the Thirties, the cartoons of big Fagans with bull shoulders, the enormous beast who used to chase Charlie Chaplin with a morphine needle, but modern, with a pea cap down over the eye and the fists clenched, the lips curled puffy to show great crooked-bit teeth fleering to fight and maul.

Out of the gang stepped Jacky Duluoz in the identical pose, hunched to bull and his face twisted and eyes popping, fists clenched; they came up against each other's noses breathing hard to hold the act, almost teeth to teeth; they'd spent countless freezing winter nights walking back from the fights and wrestling matches and movies of boyhood like this, side by side, below zero weather their mouths blowing balloons, so that people saw them with a sense of disbelief that in the dark they couldnt check, Iddyboy Joe and Zagg the two big Marines coming up the street to throw saloons to the wind. Some Melvillean dream of whaling-town streets in the New England night . . . Once Gus Rigopoulos had held complete sway and power over the soul of Iddyboy, who was a big-hearted simple stud with the power of two grown men; would dance like a witch doctor in front of him, eyes popping, in summer parks, Iddyboy in his good nature pretending to slaver at the mouth unless he actually did and do his bidding completely like a zombie, and turn on Zagg, at Gus's orders, and chase him howling like a rhinoceros bull through the jungles of the adolescent screamers in afterdark lots; a long-standing joke in the gang that Mighty Ibbyboy'd murder at G.J.'s bidding. But now they had subsided a little; Iddyboy had a girl, was on his way to see her, "Rita's her name," he told them, "you dont know her she is a nice girl, up there," pointing, telling them in his simple way, a big red-cheeked robust French Canadian paisan son of a large raucous family two blocks away. On his head too the snow had piled in a little hosanna'd crown . . . his well-combed, sleek hair, his big self-satisfied healthy face full and rich above the dark scarf and great warm coat of New England winter. "Eeedyboy!" he repeated, looking at everybody significantly, and starting off. "I see you——"

"Lookat him go, fuggen Iddyboy, d'javer see him walk home from school weekdays——"

"Hey Mouse no kiddin hear what Jack's sayin? The first guy out of high school every day, the cellar doors open, the bell's just rung, everybody went back to home room, here comes Iddyboy, man number one, just like a dream he flies out walking long and with big lumberjack steps he cuts over the grass, the sidewalk, the canal bridge, right by the lunchcart, the tracks, the city hall, now here comes the first high school regular kid out the cellar door, Jimmy McFee, Joe Rigas, me, the fast ones, out we come a hundred yards behind Iddyboy—"

"Iddyboy's already halfway up Moody Street, he not only wants to get to his homework as soon as possible because it takes him six hours to get it—"

"—flying on fast feet he strides past the Silver Star saloon, the big tree in front the girls' school, the statue, the—"

"—here he is"—(Lauzon and Zagg now vying to scream these informations to G.J. and all the others)—"six hours to get it done his homework but he has to eat his three hamburgers before supper and play six games of pish nut with Terry his sister—"

"—no time for any old Iddyboy to hang around and have a smoke and talk in front of high school and let Joe Maple see him and report him to the headmaster, Iddyboy the most honest hardworking never-played-hooky-in-his-life student in United States of America is leading the parade home up Moody . . . Long after him come the girls with their ga-dam bandanas and bananas. . . ."

"—Whattaguy that Iddyboy! There he goes in the snow." G.J. had taken up and was pointing him out. "See the snow hides his ass now. . . . Eeedy-bye oo You Babe OObloo is the salt of the earth, the top of the soup, the—no shit the finest kid that ever walked this God's green if we're gonna be ever saved . . . A little peace before we die, dear Lord," said G.J., concluding, making the sign of the cross, as everybody looked at him out of the corners of their eyes for the next laugh.

And the bright and merry corner was all theirs for a fifteen-minute interlude standing and talking in the youth of their hometown days. "Whattaya say there Zagg," said G.J., suddenly and roughly he grabbed Zagg and pulled him down into a headlock and rubbed his hair and laughed. "Good old Zagg, all the time he's standin there with a big smile on his face . . . what a good kid you are Zaggo— Scotty never had more gold in his teeth with his Kid Faro dealings than you in your cracky cock-eyed always down in the mouth eyes shine to show Zagg, that's no kidding Zagg . . . In the interests of which, burp, brup," lifting his leg several times in a lewd meaning, "I shall have to apply the headlock to you several vises tighter till you cry for mercy from Turko G.J. the Masked Ga-dam Marvel of Lowell decides to ease up and hand his mercy—back, gentlemen, while I bring Zaggo Dejesus Dulouz to his ga-dam knees once and mighty for all—"

"Look, six thousand little kids in Destouches' store buying up all the licorice and caramels—chewing stones in 'em— Comics . . . What a life when you think of it—All the little kids lined up at Boisvert's waitin for beans on Saturday night, in the cold wind, hey Mouse take it easy," Zagg said from the headlock below. They stood, all six, Zaza the funny furious rage of a cat; Vinny suddenly laughing and slapping Lousy and yelling in his rich throatbroken voice "Good old Belgium Kid Louso you sen-e-ve-bitch!"; Scotty thinking "You think they'll lend me the money and sign on the dotted line so I can get that car next summer, never"; Jack Dulouz beaming, aureating the universe in his head, eyes blazing; Mouse Rigopoulos nodding final confirmation with himself that all things would end and end very sadly; and Albert Lauzon, wise, silent, amazing, spitting soundlessly a little dry snowflake of spit through his teeth to mark the general peace, with them and without them, there and not there, child, old man, the sweetest; all six standing there, silent at last, straight-backed, looking at their Square of life. Never dreaming.

5

Never dreaming, was I, poor Jack Duluoz, that the soul is dead. That from Heaven grace descends, the ministers thereof . . . No Doctor Pisspot Poorpail to tell me; no example inside my first and only skin. That love is the heritage, and cousin to death. That the only love can only be the first iove, the only death the last, the only life within, and the only word . . . choked forever.

It was at the dance. The Rex Ballroom; with coat attendants in a drafty hall, a window, coatroom racks, fresh snow spilled on the boards; the rosy girls and handsome boys running in, the boys clacking heels, the girls in high heels, short dresses of the Thirties showing sexy legs. With awe we teenagers gave up our coats, got our brass disks, walked into the great sigh of the ballroom all six with fear, unknown sorrows. The band was on the stand, a young band, some seventeen-year-old musicians, tenors, trombones; an old pianist; a young leader; they struck up the sad lament of a ballad. *"The smoke from my cigarette climbs through the air. . . . "* The dancers met, engaged, shuffled; powder on the floor; lights playing in polkadots around the hall with its upstairs balcony where cool young sitters watched. The six boys stood at the entrance undecided, raw, foolish; turning sheepish smiles to one another for support; starting off in a halting gang, down the wall, past the wallflowers, the cold windows of winter, the seats, the other gangs of boys stiff collared and slick; the sudden group of jitterbugs with long hair and pegged pants. A bird of sadness whirled slowly around the room with the polkadots, singing love and death. . . . *"The walls of my room fade away in the blue and I'm deep in a dream of you. . . ."*

A jitterbug kid we knew was there. Whitey St. Claire from Cheever Street, long hair, pegged pants, bushy eyebrows, a strange serious interesting look, five feet tall, flashy dissipated rings under his eyes. "Oh Gene Krupa is the maddest drummer in the world! I saw him in Boston! He was the end! Look, you guys gotta learn to jitterbug! Watch!" With his little male partner Chummy Courval, who was even shorter and inconceivably sadder and more glamorous and with a button-down lounge lapel longer than almost his whole body, he joined hands and dug in heels in the floor and they flammed and whammed to show us.

Us, the gang: "What funny guys!"

"Amazing maniacs!"

"Did you hear what he said? Sixteen blondes fainted!"

"What a way to dance—I wish I could do it!"

"Now we'll get to meet some girls and throw em on the couch you babe!"

"We'll smoke them reefers and become big sex fiends you babe! Zeet?"

Whitey introduced me to Maggie. "I tried and tried to work that chick!" I saw her, standing in the crowd, forlorn, dissatisfied, dark, unpleasantly strange. Half reluctantly we were brought together and paraded to the floor arm in arm.

Maggie Cassidy—that in its time must have been Casa d'Oro—sweet, dark, rich as peaches—dim to the senses like a great sad dream—

"I suppose you're wondering what an Irish girl can be doing at a New Year's Eve dance unescorted," she said to me on the dancefloor; I, dope, had before danced only once, with Pauline Cole, high school sweetheart. ("*She'll be jealous!*" I enjoyed the thought.)

I didnt know what to say to Maggie, slavish I tied my tongue to the gate.

"Oh come on—say, you're a football player Whitey said.

"Whitey?"

"Whitey that introduced us, dummy."

It pleased me to be called a name, as though she was a younger sister—

"Do you get hurt often? my brother Roy gets hurt all the time that's why I hate football. I suppose you like it. You've got a bunch of friends. They look like a nice bunch of fellas— Do you know Jimmy Noonan in Lowell High?" She was nervous, curious, gossipy, womany: at the same time suddenly she'd caress me, say, at this early beginning, the necktie, adjust it; or push back my uncombed hair; something maternal, fleet, sorry. My hands clawed into fists to think of her when I got home that night. For, just ripened, the flesh bulged and was firm from under her shiny dress belt; her mouth pouted soft, rich, red, her black curls adorned sometimes the snow-smooth brow; up from her lips came rosy auras hinting all her health and merriness, seventeen years old. She leaned on one leg with the laze of a Spanish cat, a Spanish Carmen; she turned throwing fecund hair in quick knowing sorrying glances; she herself jeweled in the mirror; I looked blankly over her head to think of other things.

"Got a girl?"

"In high school—Pauline Cole is my girl, I met her under the clock every afternoon after third bell—" Iddyboy's rapid homeward walk now far away news in this new head of mine.

"And you tell me right away you got a girl!" Her teeth at first didnt seem attractive; her chin had a little doublechin of beauty, if the men will understand . . . that unnamed dimple chin, to perfection, and Spanish—her lip curled, slightly parted teeth charmed and enhanced sensuous, drowning lips, devourous lips; so at first you saw the little pearly teeth—

"You're probably an honest boy— You're French Canadian aintcha? I bet all the girls go for you, I bet you're gonna be a big success." I was going to grow up to walk in sleet in fields; didnt know it then.

"Oh—" blushing—"not exactly—"

"But you're only sixteen years old, you're younger than me, I'm seventeen—" She brooded and bit her rich lips: my soul began its first sink into her, deep, heady, lost; like drowning in a witches' brew, Keltic, sorcerous, starlike. "That makes me old enough ha ha," and she laughed her own incomprehensible girly jokes as I put my hard arm around her soft waist and took her dancing awkward dumb steps under the balloons and crinkly pop funhats of New

Year's Eve America and the world orange and black like the
Snow Hallowe'en, dumb and swallowing in my ignorance
and position in time— People watching us saw the girl,
timid, pretty, rather small-faced in a small hair crown but
on closer inspection cameo-like in choiceness but no paleness
eyes therein, the gimlet fires in the beauty showed; and the
boy, me, Jacky Duluoz, kid of writeups, track teams, home
and believing goodheartedness with just a touch of the Canuck half-Indian doubt and suspicion of all things non-Ca-
nuck, non-half-Indian—a lout—the order of the lout on my
arm—They saw this boy well-brushed though not combed
consciously, still a kid, suddenly big as a man, awkward,
etc.—with serious blue-eyed pensive countryboy countenance sitting in gray high school halls in button-down
sweater no water on his hair as photographer snaps line of
home roomers— Boy and girl, arms around each other,
Maggie and Jack, in the sad ball floor of life, already crest-
fallen, corners of the mouth giving up, shoulders loosening
to hang, frowns, minds forewarned—love is bitter, death
is sweet.

6

The Concord River flows by her house, in July evening the
ladies of Massachusetts Street are sitting on wooden doorsteps
with newspapers for fans, on the river the starlight shines.
The fireflies, the moths, the bugs of New England summer
rattlebang on screens, the moon looms huge and brown over
Mrs. McInerney's tree. Little Buster O'Day is coming up

the road with his wagon, torn knees, punching it through holes in the unpaved ground, the streetlamp dropping a brown vast halo bugswept on his little homeward figure. Still, and soft, the stars on the river run.

The Concord River, scene of sand embankments, railroad bridges, reeds, bullfrogs, dye mills—copses of birch, vales, in winter the dreaming white—but now in July midsummer the stars roll vast and shiny over its downward flow to the Merrimack. The railroad train crashes over the bridges; the children beneath, among the tar poles, are swimming naked. The engine's fire glow is red as it goes over, flares of deep hell are thrown on the little figures. Maggie is there, the dogs are there, little fires . . .

The Cassidys live on Massachusetts Street at No. 31— it's a wood house, seven rooms, apple tree in back; chimney; porch, with screen, and swing; no sidewalk; rickety fence against which in June tall sunflowers lean at noon for wild and tender hallucinations of little infants playing there with wagons. The father James Cassidy is an Irishman, brakeman on the Boston and Maine; soon conductor; the mother, a former O'Shaughnessy with dove's eyes still in her long-lost face of love now face of life.

The river comes between lovely shores narrowing. Bungalows scatter the landscape. The tannery's over to the west. Little grocery stores with wood fences and dusty paths, grass, some drying-out wood at noon, the ring ding of the little bell, kids buying Bostons or penny Bolsters at lunch noon; or milk early Saturday morning when all is so blue and sweet for the day of the play. Cherry trees drops blossoms in May. The funny gladness of the cat rubbing against the porch steps in the drowsy two o'clock when Mrs. Cassidy with her littlest daughter returns from shopping at Kresge's downtown, gets off the bus at the junction, walks seven houses down Massachusetts Street with her bundles, the ladies see her, call out "What'd you buy Mrs. Cassidy? Is that fire sale still on at Giant store?"

"Radio says it is . . ." another greeter.

"Wasnt you on the Strand program on the sidewalk interviews?—Tom Wilson asked the silliest questions—Hee hee hee!"

Then among themselves "That little girl must have rickets the way she walks—"

"Those cakes she gave me yesterday I just had to throw them away—"

And the sun beams gladly on the woman at the gate of her house. "Now where can Maggie be? I told her a dozen times I wanted that wash hung out before I got back even if it was eleven o'clock—"

And at night the river flows, it bears pale stars on the holy water, some sink like veils, some show like fish, the great moon that once was rose now high like a blazing milk flails its white reflection vertical and deep in the dark surgey mass wall river's grinding bed push. As in a sad dream, under the streetlamp, by pocky unpaved holes in dirt, the father James Cassidy comes home with lunchpail and lantern, limping, redfaced, and turns in for supper and sleep.

Now a door slams. The kids have rushed out for the last play, the mothers are planning and slamming in kitchens, you can hear it out in swish leaf orchards, on popcorn swings, in the million-foliaged sweet wafted night of sighs, songs, shushes. A thousand things up and down the street, deep, lovely, dangerous, aureating, breathing, throbbing like stars; a whistle, a faint yell; the flow of Lowell over rooftops beyond; the bark on the river, the wild goose of the night yakking, ducking in the sand and sparkle; the ululating lap and purl and lovely mystery on the shore, dark, always dark the river's cunning unseen lips murmuring kisses, eating night, stealing sand, sneaky.

"Mag-gie!" the kids are calling under the railroad bridge where they've been swimming. The freight train still rumbles over a hundred cars long, the engine threw the flare on little white bathers, little Picasso horses of the night as dense and tragic in the gloom comes my soul looking for what was there that disappeared and left, lost, down a path— the gloom of love. Maggie, the girl I loved.

7

In winter night Massachusetts Street is dismal, the ground's frozen cold, the ruts and pock holes have ice, thin snow slides over the jagged black cracks. The river is frozen to stolidity, waits; hung on a shore with remnant show-off boughs of June— Ice skaters, Swedes, Irish girls, yellers and singers—they throng on the white ice beneath the crinkly stars that have no altar moon, no voice, but down heavy tragic space make halyards of Heaven on in deep, to where the figures fantastic amassed by scientists cream in a cold mass; the veil of Heaven on tiaras and diadems of a great Eternity Brunette called night.

Among these skaters Maggie performed; in her sweet white skates, white muff, you see the flash of her eye in

their pools of darkness all the more strikingly: the pinkness
of her cheek, her hair, the crown of her eyes corona'd by
God's own bent wing— For all I knew as I toasted my
skated feet at Concord River fires in the February Lowell,
Maggie could have been the mother or the daughter of
God—

Dirty snow piled in the gutters of Massachusetts Street,
something forlorn hid in little pits of dirt, dark—the mute
companions of my midnight walks from the overpowering
lavish of her kisses.

She gave me a kiss upsidedown in the chair, it was a
winter night not long after I'd met her, I was in the dark
room with the big radio with its throbbish big brown dial
that Vinny also had in his house and I'm rocking in the
chair, Mrs. Cassidy her mother is in her own kitchen the
way my mother three miles across town was—same old big
old good old Lowell lady in her eternity wiping the dishes
putting them away in the clean cupboards with that little
feminate neatness and orderly ideas of how to go about
things—Maggie's on the porch goofing in the icy night a
minute with Bessy Jones her chum from the bungalow across
the street, a big fat red-haired goodnatured girl with freckles
and whose inconceivably feeble little brother sometimes
delivered me notes from Maggie written the night before
school in some brown light of her bedroom or in the morning
at pipe keen frost, to hand to him, over the crackly fence,
and he in his usual round of days trudged to school two
miles away or took the bus and as he rheumy-eyedly weep-
ingly came into his Spanish class which was every morning
the second and impossibly dull he handed me the note
sometimes with a feeble little joke—just a little kid, for

some reason they'd shoved him on to high school through red morning cold parochials where he skipped grades and missed the sixth, or fifth, or both, and here he was a little kid with a hunting rag cap with a Scottish haggle tassel and we believed him to be like our age. Maggie would plant the note in his thin freckly hand, Bessy'd be giggling from behind the open kitchen window, she's taking advantage of the window being open and also putting the empty milk-bottles out. Little Massachusetts Street in the cold mornings of rosy snow sun in January is alive with the fragrant whip of blacksmoke from all the cottage chimneys; on the white frozen cap of the Concord River we see last night's bonfire a charred ruinous black spot near the thin bare reddish reeds of the other shore; the whistle of the Boston and Maine engine sounds across the trees, you shudder and pull your coat tighter to hear it. Bessy Jones . . . sometimes she'd write notes to me too, giving instructions on how to win Maggie, that Maggie'd also read. I accepted everything.

"Maggie loves you," etc., "she's madder about you than I can ever remember her being mad about anybody else" and in effect she'd say "Maggie loves you, but dont try her patience—tell her you want to marry her or sumptin." Young girls—giggly—on the porch—as I sit in the living-room dark waiting for Maggie to come back on the chair with me. My tired track team legs are beneath me, folded. I hear other voices on the Cassidy porch, some boys, that Art Swenson I heard about—I feel jealousy but it's only the bare beginning of all the jealousy that came later. I'm waiting for Maggie to come and kiss me, make it official. While waiting I have ample time to review our love affair; how the first night she'd meant nothing to me when we danced,

I held her, she seemed small, thin, dark, unsubstantial, not important enough—Just her strange rare sadness coming from the other side of something made me barely notice she was there: her pretty looks . . . all girls had pretty looks, even G.J. hadnt mentioned her. . . . The profundity wave of her womanhood had not yet settled over me. That was New Year's Eve—after the dance we'd walked home in the cold night, the snow was over, just tight and soft on the implacable frozen ground, we passed long construction oil flares like avenues and parades on our way down to South Lowell and the banks of the Concord—the silent frost on the rooftops in the starlight, ten degrees above zero. "Sit on the porch awhile anyway—" There were little children-whimpering understandings between us that we would join our lips and kiss even if we had to do it outdoors—The thought of it had begun to excite me even then. But now, waiting in the chair, and why worry about time, the meaning of her *kissed* had become all things to me. In the variety of the tone of her words, moods, hugs, kisses, brushes of the lips, and this night the upside-down kiss over the back of the chair with her dark eyes heavy hanging and her blushing cheeks full of sweet blood and sudden tenderness brooding like a hawk over the boy over the back, holding the chair on both sides, just an instant, the startling sudden sweet fall of all her hair over my face and the soft downward brush of her lips, a moment's penetration of sweet lip flesh, a moment's drowned in thinking and kissing in it and praying and hoping and in the mouth of life when life is young to burn cool skin eye-blinking joy—I held her captured upside down, also for just a second, and savored the kiss which first had surprised me like blind man's bluff so I didnt know really who was kissing me for the very first instant but now I knew and knew everything more than ever, as, grace-wise, she descended to me from the upper dark where I'd thought only cold could be and with all her heavy lips and breast in my neck and on my head and sudden fragrance of the night brought with her from the porch, of some 5 & 10 cheap perfumes of herself the little hungry scent of perspiration warm in her flesh like preciousness.

I held her a long time, even when she struggled to fall back. I realized she'd done it for a mood. She loved me. Also I think we were both frightened later when we'd hold a kiss for 35 minutes until the muscles of our lips would get cramps and it was painful to go on—but somehow we were supposed to do this, and what everybody said, the other kids, Maggie and all the others "necking" at skate and post office parties and on porches after dances had learned this was the thing—and did it in spite of how they felt about it personally—the fear of the world, the children clinging in what they think is a mature, secure kiss (challenging and grown-up)—not understanding joy and personal reverence— It's only later you learn to lean your head in the lap of God, and rest in love. Some gigantic sexual drive was behind these futile long smooches, sometimes our teeth'd grind, our mouths burn from interchanged spittle, our lips blister, bleed, chap— We were scared.

I lay there on my side with my arm around her neck, my hand gripped on her rib, and I ate her lips and she mine. There were interesting crises. . . . No way to go further without fighting. After that we'd just sit and gab in the black of the parlor while the family slept and the radio played low. One night I heard her father come in the kitchen door—I had no idea then of the great fogs rolling over fields by the sea in Nova Scotia and the poor little cottages in lost storms, sad work, wintry work in the bottom of life, the sad men with pails who walk in fields—the new form of the sun every morning— Ah I loved my Maggie, I wanted to eat her, bring her home, hide her in the heart of my life the rest of my days. I prayed in Sainte Jeanne d'Arc church for the grace of her love; I'd almost forgotten . . .

Let me sing the beauty of my Maggie. Legs:—the knees attached to the thighs, knees shiny, thighs like milk. Arms:—the levers of my content, the serpents of my joy. Back:—the sight of that in a strange street of dreams in the middle of Heaven would make me fall sitting from glad recognition. Ribs?—she had some melted and round like a well formed apple, from her thigh bones to waist I saw the earth roll. In her neck I hid myself like a lost snow goose of Australia, seeking the perfume of her breast. . . . She didnt let me, she was a good girl. The poor big alley cat with her, though almost a year younger, had black ideas about her legs that he hid from himself, also in his prayers didnt mention . . . the dog. Across the big world darkness I've come, in boat, in bus, in airplane, in train standing my shadow immense traversing the fields and the redness of engine boilers behind me making me omnipotent upon the earth of the night, like God—but I have never made love with a little finger that has won me since. I gnawed her face with my eyes; she loved that; and that was bastardly I didnt know she loved me—I didnt understand.

"Jack—," after we'd had all our conversations about the kids she fiddled with all day, while I was at school and since I'd last seen her, the gossip, things of high school kids talking about others their age, the stories, rumors, news of the dance, of marriage . . . "Jack, marry me some day."

"Yes, yes, always—nobody else."

"You sure there's nobody else?"

"Well *who* could be?" I didnt love the girl Maggie was jealous of, Pauline, who'd found me standing in the gang of football players one night in autumn at a dance where I'd gone because there was a banquet for the players and a basketball game we wanted to see, boy stuff—I was waiting in the corner for the dance to end, the idea of dancing with a girl was impossible but I had it concealed— She picked me out of a corner like young men dream. She said, "Hey I like you!—you're bashful, I like bashful people!" and drew me tremblingly excitingly to the floor, great eyes in mine, and pulled my body and hers and squeezed me interestingly and made me "dance" to talk, to get acquainted—the smell of her hair was killing me! In her door at home she was looking at me with the moon in her eyes, saying, "If you wont kiss me I'll kiss you" and opened the screendoor I'd just closed and gave me a cool kiss— We had talked about kisses looking at each other's mouths all night; we had said we werent interested in such things—"I'm a good girl, I believe in h-hmmm—kissing"—flutter—"but I mean I wouldnt allow anything beyond that to happen"—like in New England the girls—"but you've got bedroom eyes, hey. Did I tell ya about the guy I didnt know who put his arm around me at the Girl Officers' Ball?" She was a Girl Officer.

"What?"

"Dont you want to know if I asked him to take his hands off me—?"

"Yeah?"

"Dont be silly, I dont talk to strangers."

Pauline, brown hair, blue eyes, the great glistening stars in her lips— She too lived near a river, the Merrimack, but near the highway, the big bridge, the big carnival and football field—you could see the factories across the river. I spent many afternoons there conversing with her in the snow, about kisses, before meeting Maggie. All of a sudden one night she opens the damned door and kisses me—big stuff! The first night I met her all I could do was smell her hair in my bed, in my hair—told this to Lousy, I smelt her in his hair too. It interested Lousy. When I told him we'd finally kissed the night before (sitting with him on my bed with the gang G.J. Scotty Iddyboy sitting in chairs of my bedroom after supper talking about the team my mother doing the dishes my father at the radio) Lousy wanted me to kiss him like I had kissed Pauline. We did it, too; the others didnt even stop talking about the team. But now Maggie was another matter—her kisses, an expensive wine, we dont have much, nor often—hidden in the earth—limited, like Napoleon brandy—pretty soon no more. Marry, love somebody else? Impossible. "I love only you, Maggie," I tried to say, no more success than with G.J. the little boy loves of puberty. I tried to assure her that she would never have cause for jealousy, truly. Enough of singing— I'll sing later—the story of Maggie—the beginning of my jealousy, the things that happened.

The mortality in my heart is heavy, they're going to throw me in a hole already eaten by the dogs of dolor like a sick Pope who's played with too many young girls the black tears flowing from his skeleton-hole eyes.

Ah life, God—we wont find them any more the Nova
Scotias of flowers! No more saved afternoons! The shadows,
the ancestors, they've all walked in the dust of 1900 seeking
the new toys of the twentieth century just as Céline says—
but it's still love has found us out, and in the stalls was
nothing, eyes of drunken wolves was all. Ask the guys at
the war.

8

I see her head bowed in thinking of me, by the river, her
beautiful eyes searching inside for the proper famous thought
of me she loved. Ah my angel—my new angel, black, follows
me now—I exchanged the angel of life for the other. Before
the crucifix of Jesus in the house I stood attentively, sure
of many things, I was going to see the tears of God and
already I saw them in that countenance elongated white in
plaster that gave life—gave life bitten, finished, droop-eyed,
the hands nailed, the poor feet also nailed, folded, like
winter cold feet of the poor Mexican worker you see in the
street waiting for the guys to come with the barrels to empty
the rags the crap and keeps one foot on the other to keep
warm— Ah— The head bent, like the moon, like my picture
of Maggie, mine and God's; the dolors of a Dante, at sixteen,
when we dont know conscience or what we're doing.

When I was younger, ten, I'd pray at the crucifix for the
love of my Ernie Malo, a little boy in parochial school, son
of a judge, who because he was like my dead brother Gerard
I loved with as sublime a love—with the strangeness of

childhood in it, for instance I'd pray at the picture of my
brother Gerard, dead at nine when I was four, to insure the
friendship, respect and grace of Ernie Malo—I wanted little
Ernie to give me his hand, simply, and say to me, "Ti Jean,
you you're nice!" And—"Ti Jean, we'll be friends always,
we'll go hunting together in Africa when we finish school
ha?" I found him as beautiful as seven times the pick because
his rosy cheeks and white teeth and the eyes of a woman
dreaming, of an angel maybe, bit my heart; children love
each other like lovers, we dont look at their little dramas
in the course of our adult days. The picture—, also at the
crucifix I prayed. Every day at school it was one ruse after
another to make me loved by my boy; I watched him when
we all stood in line in the schoolyard, the Brother up front
was delivering his speech, his prayer in the cold zero, redness
of Heaven behind him, the big steam and balloon and
ballturd of horses in the little alley that crossed the school
property (Saint Joseph's Parochial), the ragmen were coming
at the same time we were marching to class. Dont think
we werent afraid! They had greasy hats, they grinned in
dirty holes on top of tenements. . . . I was crazy then, my
head ran fantastic ideas from seven morning till ten night
like a little Rimbaud in his racks cracked. Ah the poetry
I'd written at ten—letters to Maggie—afternoons walking
to school I'd imagine movie cameras turned on me, the
Complete Life of a Parochial School Boy, his thoughts, way
he jumps against fences. —Voila, at sixteen, Maggie—the
crucifix—there, God knew I had love troubles that were big
and real now with his plastic statued head just neckbroke
leaned over as sad as ever, more sad than ever. "You found
yourself your little darknesses?" said God to me, silently,

with his statue head, before it my hands clasped waiting.
"Grew up with your little *gidigne?*" (dingdong). At the age
of seven a priest had asked me in the confessional "And you
played with your little *gidigne?*"

"Yes *mon père.*"

"Well therefore, if you played with your little *gidigne* say
a whole rosary and after that do ten *Notre Pères* and ten *Salut
Marie's* in front of the altar and after that you can go." The
Church carried me from one Saviour to another; who's done
that for me since?—why the tears?—God spoke to me from
the crucifix:—"Now it is morning and the good people are
talking next door and the light comes in through the shade—
my child, you find yourself in the world of mystery and
pain not understandable—I know, angel—it is for your
good, we shall save you, because we find your soul as important as the soul of the others in the world—but you must
suffer for that, in effect my child, you must die, you must
die in pain, with cries, frights, despairs—the ambiguities!
the terrors!—the lights, heavy, breakable, the fatigues,
ah—"

I listened in the silence of my mother's house to divine
how God was going to arrange the success of my love with
Maggie. Now I could see her tears too. Something there
was, that was not, nothing, just the consciousness that God
awaits us.

"Mixing up in the affairs of the world isnt for God," I
told myself hurrying to school, ready for another day.

9

Here was a typical day, I'd get up in the morning, seven, my mother'd call, I'd smell the breakfast of toast and gruel, the windows were frozen an inch of snowy ice the whole glass illuminated rose by the transformations of the ocean of winter outside. I'd jump out of the sheets so warm soft, I wanted to stay buried all day with Maggie and maybe also just the darkness and the death of *no time;* I'd jump into my incontestable clothes; inescapable cold shoes, cold socks that I threw on the oil stove to warm. Why did people stop wearing long underwear?—it's a bitch to put on little undershirts in the morning—I'd throw my warm pajamas on the bed— My room was lit by the morning the color of a rose coal a half-hour dropped from the grate, my things all there like the Victrola, the toy pool table, the toy green desk, the linoleum all raised one side and sitting on books to make banks for the pool balls and raced track meets when I had time but I didnt any more— My tragic closet, my jacket hung in a dampness like powder from fresh plaster lost locked like adobe closets Casbah roof civilizations; the papers covered with my printed handwritings, on the floor, among shoes, bats, gloves, sorrows of pasts. . . . My cat who'd slept with me all night and was now thrown awake in the empty semi-warm bed was trying to hide himself in near the pillow and sleep a little more but smelled the bacon and hurried to begin his day, to the floor, plap, disappearing like a sound with little swift feet; sometimes he was gone when seven o'clock woke me, already out making crazy little tracks in the new snow and little yellow balls of pipi and shivering his teeth to see the birds in trees as cold as iron. "Peeteepeet!" the birds said; I look outside briefly before leaving my room, in a window hole, the roofs are pure, white, the trees frozen mad, the cold houses smoking thinly, docile-eyed in winter.

You have to put up with life.

10

In the tenement it was high, you could see downstairs the roofs of Gardner Street and the big field and the trail people used gray rose dawns five o'clock January to go flatulate in church. There were old women of the block who went to church every dawn, and late afternoon; and sometimes again evening; old, prayery, understanding of something that little children dont understand and in their tragedy so close you'd think to the tomb that you saw already their profiles sitting in rose satin the color of their rose-morns of life and expectoration but the scent of other things rising from the hearts of flowers that die at the end of autumn and we've thrown them on the fence. It was the women of interminable novenas, lovers of funerals, when somebody died they knew it right away and hurried to church, to the house of death and to the priest possibly; when they themselves died the other old women did the same thing, it was the cups of sugar in eternity— There's the trail; and winter important morning opening stores and people *hallo!* and I go ready to go to school. It's a *méli-mélon* of morning everywhere.

11

I'd have breakfast.

My father was usually away on his out-of-town job running a linotype for some printer—Andover, near the little crew-cuts there who had no idea of the darkness inherent in the earth if they didnt see that sad big man crossing the night to go make his 40-hour week—so he was not at our kitchen table, usually just my mother, cooking, and my sister, getting ready for her job at So and So's or *The Citizen*, she was a bookbinder—Grave facts of worklife were explained to me but I was too proud in purple love to listen— Ahead of me, nothing but the New York *Times*, Maggie, and the great world night and morning of the shrouds on twig and leaf, by lakes—"Ti Jean!" they called me—I was a big lout, ate enormous breakfasts, suppers, afternoon snacks (milk, one quart: peanut butter and crackers, ½ pound). "Ti Jean!"—when my father was home, *"Ti Pousse!"* he called me, chuckling (Little Thumb). Now oatmeal breakfasts in the rosiness—

"Well how's your love affair with Maggie Cassidy coming along?" my sister'd ask, grinning from behind a sandwich, "or did she give you the air because of Moe Cole!"

"You mean Pauline? Why Pauline?"

"You dont know how jealous women get—that's all they think about— You'll see—"

"I dont see anything."

"Tiens," my mother's saying, "here's some bacon with toast I made a big batch this morning because yesterday you finished em all up and you was fightin at the end for the

46

last time like you used to do over Kremel, never mind the
jealous girls and the tennis courts, it's gonna be awright
if you just stick to your guns there like a real French Canadian
boy the way I brought you up to respect decency—listen,
Ti Jean, you'll never be sorry if you always follow a clean
life. You dont have to believe me, you know." And she'd
sit and we'd all eat. At the last minute I'd stand undecided
in my room, looking at the little radio I just got and in
which I'd just started listening to Glenn Miller and Jimmy
Dorsey and romantic songs that tore my heart out . . . *My
Reverie, Heart and Soul,* Bob Eberle, Ray Eberle, all the blue
sighing America was racked up behind me in the night that
was all mine and the glory of the tenderness of the trembling
kiss of Maggie and all love as only teenagers know it and
like perfect blue ballrooms. I wrung my hands Shakespear-
eanly at my closet door; crossing the bathroom to grab a
towel my eyes misted from sudden romantic notions of
myself sweeping Maggie off a pink dancefloor onto a pier
with a moon shining, into a slick convertible, a close kiss
long and sincere (just a little to the right).

I'd just started shaving; one night my sister had surprised
me combing my hair making a little tuck in my crown for
a wave—"Oh boy, look at the Romeo!" It was surprising;
two months before I'd been a boy, coming home from fall
football practice in iron dusks wrapped in my jacket and
earmuff cap, bent, offnights I'd spot pins at the alley with
twelve-year-old boys, at three cents a string—20 strings,
60 cents, usually I made that or a buck— Just a boy, I'd
only recently cried because I lost my hat while playing in
a WPA League basketball game won at the last second by
a sensational toss by Billy Artaud almost rivaling the time

at the Boys' Club tie-score with one second to go against
a Greek team tigrishly named I made a one-hand last-whistle
jump shot out of the scrambling pack from about the foul
line and the ball hung in the basket a horrid second for
everybody to see, bagged, the game over, Zagg and his
tricks—an inborn showman—everlasting hero. The hat now
forgotten.

"By Ma," kissing my mother on the cheek, starting off
for school, she herself worked part time in the shoe factory
with her grave sense of life sitting grim and tireless at the
skiving machine holding stubborn shoe leathers to a blade,
her fingertips blackened, years on end of it from fourteen
on, other girls like her up and down the machines—the
whole family working, 1939 was a tail-end Depression year
about to be overshadowed by events in Poland.

I got my lunch, prepared the night before by Ma, slices
of bread and butter; nothing was more delicious than these
slices at noon after four hours almost interesting sunny
classroom absorbed in personalities of teachers like Joe Maple
with his eloquent statements in English 3 or old Mrs.
McGillicuddy the astronomy (inseparable)—bread and butter and delicious, hot mashed potatoes, nothing else, at the
roaring basement tables my lunch cost 10¢ a day— The
pièce de résistance was my magnificent chocolate-covered
ice cream stick, everyone in school 95% licked on them
greedily every noon, on benches, in the huge cellar halls,
on the sidewalks—recess—I'd sometimes in my grace like
the grace that got me Maggie get thick ice cream almost
an inch wide, by some mistake in the ice cream factory with
rich unbelievable thick chocolate layer that also by mistake
was larded and curled right on—by same industrial per-

chance, I'd get feeble anemic sticks a half-inch, already half
melted, paper-thin chocolate falling on the sidewalk of Kirk
Street as we'd Harry McCarthy, Lousy, Bill Artaud and me
lick our sticks ceremoniously greedy in the winter sun my
mind a million miles from romance— So I'd bring my bread
and butter lunch, to be stuffed quickly in my homeroom
desk—kiss Mother—and take off, on foot, to stride as fast
as I could, like everybody else, down Moody past the posts
of Textile to the great bridge to Moody tenements and down
the hill into the city, gray, prosperous, puffing in the morn.
And along the way the soldiers'd fall in, G.J. off Riverside
going to his business course in Lowell High where he learned
typing and bookkeeping and made fantasies around the lus-
cious girls who were going to be sexy secretaries, he'd begun
wearing necktie and suit, he'd say "Zagg that Miss Gordon
is going to take that expression of cool indifference off her
face one of these days and let her panties slip on the floor
for me, mark my words—and it'll be in one of those empty
rooms one of these afternoons"—but instead of actual sexual
conquests he'd wind up at two in the afternoon with his
books in the Rialto B movie—alone, faced by the reality
of Franchot Tone and Bruce Cabot and Alice Faye and Don
Ameche grinning smiling at Tyrone etc. and old men and
old women living on relief wide-eyed in the show. Too,
Lousy'd come angling to my walk from Riverside; then,
incredibly, Billy Artaud'd overtake us all from the rear
striding madly down from the upper outskirt hill of Moody
and just as we reached the canal downtown we'd see all of
us that Iddyboy was way ahead and was already leaning out
of his freshman homeroom window dutifully obeying the
teacher's request to open window—"Eeediboy!" he'd yell,

and disappear in, he was the most willing student in LHS and had the lowest marks and otherwise he would have been able to play football and would have killed everybody broken Malden guards in half with one clip of his granite elbow— Open homeroom window in Lowell, rose morn and birds upon the Boott Mill canal— Later it was going to be the open window morn at Columbia University the pigeonshit on the sill of Mark Van Doren and the Shakespeare of drunken sleeps under an Avon apple tree, ah—

Down Moody we'd sweep, primish, young, mad. Crossing us like a streamlet were the Bartlett Junior High School kids taking the riverbank route to the White Bridge and Wannalancitt Street which'd been our route for "How many years Mouse? Remember the winter it was so cold they had frostbites in the Principal's office with doctors?—"

"And the time we had that snowball war on Wannalancitt—"

"The crazy guys come to school with bikes, no kiddin Louse they had more trouble going up that hill from side to side than if they'd walk—"

"I used to walk home every noon me and Eddy Desmond wrapped in each other's arms falling on the ground—he was the laziest guy in the world, he didnt want to go to school in the afternoon, he wanted me to throw him in the river, I had to carry him—sleepy, he was like my cat, crazy—"

"Ah the old days!" Mouse'd pout black and brooding. "All I ask is a chance in this ga-dam world to earn a decent living and support my mother and see that all her needs are answered—"

"Where's Scotty workin now?"

"Didnt you hear?—out in Chelmsford, they're building

a big war airplane base, Scotty and all the old WPA bums
go out and dig up trees and cut em down and clear the
ground—he's making a million dollars a week—he gets up
at four o'clock in the morning—Fuggen Scotcho—I love
Scotcho— Dont catch *him* going to no high school and
no business school courses, Kid Faro wants his money
now—"

We came to the bridge. The winter trickle between the
jagged canyons of rock below, the pools of ice formed, rosy
matin on the froth of little rapids, cold—far off, the bungalows of Centreville, and the snowy hump meadow, and
hints of New Hampshire forests deep in where big men in
mackinaws now with axes and boots and cigarettes and
laughs drove old Reos through rutted dirt strips among
pinestumps, to the house, the shack, the dream of wild New
England in our hearts—

"You're quiet, Zagg—that damn Maggie Cassidy's got
you boy, s'got you boy!"

"Dont let no broad get you, Zagg—love aint worth it—
what's love, *nothin.*" G.J. was against it. Not Lousy.

"No, love is *great* Mouse—something to think about—
go to church and pray Zagg You Babe! Marry her! Screw
her! Zeet? Have a good one for me!"

"Zagg," advised Gus seriously, "screw her then leave her
take it from an old seadog,—women are no good, forever
'tis written in the stars— Ah!" turning away, black—"Kick
em in the pants, put em in their place—There's enough
misery in this world, laugh, cry, sing, tomorrow is nothing— Dont let her get you down, Zagguth."

"I wont, Mouso."

"Zeet! Look here comes Billy Artaud—already for another

day rubbing his hands together—" Sure enough Billy Artaud who lived with his mother and every morning didnt rise from his bed but leaped out grinning came up rubbing his hands, you could hear the cold wiry sound of his zeal across the street.

"Hey, you guys, wait up— Let the chess champion walk!"

"You're the chess champion? Ho Ho."

"What?—"

"With my bombarding tactics I can beat you all—"

"Zeet? Look at his books!"

—Wrangling, goofing, we stride without physical pause to school past Saint Jean Baptiste Church ponderous Chartres Cathedral of the slums, past gas stations, tenements, Vinny Bergeracs— ("Fuggen Vinny's still sleepin . . . they wouldnt even take him in vocational school . . . all this morning he'll read Thrilling True Love stories and eat them Drake's Devil Cakes with the white cream in the middle . . . he never eats food, he lives on cakes. . . . Ah ga-dammit I know we played hooky yesterday but my soul cries out for Vinny this gray sad morning."

"We better be careful—two days in a row?"

"Did you hear him yestiddy?—he said he was going to get sexmad now and stick his head in the toilet bowl!")— past the City Hall, the library in back with already some old bums gathering smoking butts at the door of the newspaper room waiting for nine o'clock opening time—past Prince Street ("Zowie, only last summer think of the games we had there, Zagg, the homeruns, the triples, the great Scotch pitching shutouts—life is so *big!*")—("life my dear Lousy is immerelensum!")—past the YWCA, the canal bridge, the entrance street to the great cotton mills with all up down the morning-rosy cobbles the tight serried Colonial doors of a mid-nineteenth-century housing block for textile workers celebrated in some of Dickens' memoirs, the sad crapulous look of old redbrick sagging doorfronts and almost a century of work in the mills, gloom in the night.

And we came then mixing into the hundreds of students milling around the high school sidewalks and lawns waiting for the first bell which would be not heard outside but announced from within in a rumbling desperate-faced flying rumor so that sometimes when I was nightmarishly late I hurried all alone across the great deserted spaces only minutes ago scene of hundredfold grabbings now mopped out clean all the principals cubby-holed inside the silent high school windows in the morning's first classes, a mortifying great space of guilts, many times dreamed, sidewalk, grass. "I'm going back to school," dreams the old invalid in his innocent pillow, blind of time.

12

The class filed into school at 7:50 A.M., generally things rammed and slammed for the last time in strange antenna'd moments when nobody was saying a word and the edge of the bench was cutting my elbow as I leaned my head on it trying to catch some sleep—in the afternoon I really slept, with great success in homeroom study after one o'clock when not spitballs but love notes were thrown around—late in the school day— Sun morning was orange fire in the un-

washed windows, making way for day blue gold as birds
whistled in trees, an old man leaned on the canal rail with
his pipe in his mouth, and the canal flowed— All whorly
and whirlpools and dense and tragic and to be seen from
half a hundred windows of the north side of the high school
building, the new one and the old for freshmen. Gigantic,
the drownings in that canal would bloat a book, bloat a
page, imaginary, dream'd in that clock hour of the rosy
jongling lip of kid days in stylish sweaters. Lousy was in
his class, all was right with the world. He abhorred and
grinned on his end of a bench in the flaming sun atmospheres
of the southwest windows, which in the winter received pale
tropical flame from old northeast—the eraser's set out, the
personal face-type's got his desk, he hangles and grows
frowzy, somebody's got to set him right, the yawning day's
just begun. Magazines, peeking at them a minute in his
desk box, the lid up—"Oh there in the hall goes Mr. Nedick
the English teacher with the oversized pants—Mrs. Faherty
the freshman grade or 9th grade teacher of Shakespearean
rhymes'll come among us, there she is, the big important
tack-tock of her biglady high heels," Joycean imaginings
fill all our minds as we sit there goofily self-enduring the
morning, waiting for the grave to lean our heads in, not
knowing. In the cobbles by the factory by the canal I understand future dreams. I'll have them later on of the redbrick
mills beyond vacant canals in blue morning, the loss brow-
banging, done with— My birds will twitter on the branch
of other things.

Eyes of pretty brunettes, blondes and redheads of the
Lowell Prime are all around me. A new day in school,
everybody wide-awake looking everywhere; today 17,000

notes will be delivered from shivering hand to hand in this
ecstatic mortality. I can already see Stendhalian plots forming in the frowns of pretty girls, "Today, I'll keep that
damn Beechly awful innerested in a little idee of mine"—
like Date-with-Judies self-communing monologues—"bring
my brother into it and then everything'll be set." Others
not plotting, waiting, dreaming the enormous sad dream
of high school deaths you die at sixteen.

"Lissen, Jim, tell Bob I didnt *mean*—he knows it!"

"Sure, I told you I would!"

Running for vice-president of the sophomore class, pin-
ning photos to crucial letters, rounding up a gang, trying
to get something on Annie Kloos. They're all talking anxiously their plots, across the aisles, up and down the benches;
the hubbub is so fantastic uproar momentous, weird, like
sudden roars of Friday Afternoon California High School
Football Games over quiet bungalow roofs, like teenagers
at a roller derby, the teacher even is amazed and tries to
hide behind the New York *Times* bought on Kearney Square
at the only place where you can get them. The whole class
invincible, the teacher'll get the authority at exactly the
time but better not interfere before overtime starts—"Gonna
by golly—" "well gee—" "Hey—" "What you say there!"
"Hi!" "Dotty?—didnt I tell you that dress would look
divine?"

"You didnt miss a trick, honey, I was perfect."

"The girls were wild about it, all of them. You shoulda
heard Freda Ann come on! Yerr!"

"Freda Ann?" primping her hair very significantly. "Tell
Freda Ann she can go along her own way I can get along
without her comments—"

"Oh along along. Down in the hall's my brother Jimmy. He's got that little dumb Jones kid with him?" They join and peek, lip to ear. "See Duluoz up there? He's bringing a note from Mag-gie Cassidy."

"Who? *Mag-gie Cassi-dy?*" And they double and squeal and laugh and everybody turns to look, what are they laughing about, teacher's about to slap for order—the girls are laughing. My ears burn. I turn my dreamy inattention on everybody, thinking about my hot date pie with whipped cream last Sunday—the girls are looking into my blue windows for romance.

"Hmm. Isnt he dreamy?"

"I dont know. He looks sleepy all the time."

"That's the way I like—"

"Oh get away—how do you know how you like?"

"Wouldnt you like to know? Ask—"

"Ask *who?*"

"Ask who went with Freda Ann to the Girl Officers' Ball last Thursday and found themselves all tangled up, with Lala Duvalle and her gang of cutthroats and fingernail scratchers and you know who and know what else? I'm— Oh, here's the silence."

Blam, blam, the old teacher bangs her ruler and stands, very matronly, like an old busdriver, surveying the class for absences and then she makes a note and a few quibblings then from next room walks in Mr. Grass for some special news and everybody bends an ear as they whisper up front, a spitball sails funnily in the bright nice sun, and on comes the day. The bell. We all rush off to our first classes. Ah inconceivably lost the corridors of that long school, those long courses, the hours and semesters I missed, I played hooky two times a week on the average— Guilt. I never got over it— Classes in English . . . reading the very solid poetry of Edwin Arlington Robinson, Robert Frost and Emily Dickinson: a name I never knew to reckon with Shakespeare's. Wonderful classes in some kind of pre-science fiction astronomy, with an old lady with a long stick demonstrating moons at the blackboard. A class in physics, here we were blearily lost trying to spell the word barometer on our gray blue-lined examination paper let alone Galileo. A course in this, that, hundreds of beautiful intelligent young people hung on pursuits of pure mental interest and social jawbones, all they gotta do is get up in the morning, school takes care of the rest of their day, taxpayers support.

Some of them preferred rides to the country in tragic rumble seats, we never saw them again, they were swallowed in reform schools and marriage.

It being winter, I wore my football sweater letter "L"— to show off—it was huge, uncomfortable, too hot, I hung braced in its horrible corset of wool for hours on end day after day. Finally I settled to just my own blue home sweater buttoned down in front.

13

The second class was the Spanish one where I found the notes from Maggie, two a week. I read it right away:

Well I suppose you thought I would never write a note this week. Well I had a swell time in Boston Saturday with my mother and

sister. My little silly sister is a little flirt. I dont know what she will
be like when she grows up. Well what have you been up to since
I saw you. My brother and June that are getting married in April
were here last night. How is school? Roy Walters is at the Commodore
Tuesday and I am going. Glenn Miller is coming later on. Did you
go to the diner after you left me Sunday? Well I havent any more
to say now so

                                        So-Long MAGGIE.

Even if I was supposed to see her that night I still had
a long way to go—after school it was track, til 6, 7 P.M.
when it was my custom to walk home one mile with stiff
legs. Track was in a low vast building across the street,
with steel beams bare in the ceiling, great basketball floors
six of them, then drill floor of the High School Regiments
and sometimes several indoor football drills and some rainy
day March baseball practice and big track meets with crowds
sitting in bleachers around. Before going there I hung out
at the empty halls, classrooms—sometimes met Pauline Cole
under the clock which I'd done every day in December but
now it was January. "There you are!" She gave out with a
big smile, eyes big, moist, beautifully blue, full big lips
over great white teeth, very affectionate—it was all I could
do—"Where you been keepin yourself hey." Liking her,
liking life too, I had to stand there assuming for myself all
the gloomy guilts of the soul, out the other end of which
my life flowed crying emptying in the dark anyway—weep-
ing for what had been supposed—nothing within me to
right the wronged, no hope of hope, blear, all sincerity
crowded out by world-crowded actual people and events and
the slack watery weakness of my own mean resolution—
hung—dead—low.

Heirs leap screeching from doctors' laps while the old and

the poor die on, and who's to bend over their bed and comfort.

"Oh I have to go to track in a minute—"

"Hey can I go see you Saturday night against Worcester?—of course I'm coming anyhow, I'm only asking your permission so you'll talk to me."

O Wounded Wolfe! (That's what I thought I was, with the reading of a few books later)— At night I closed my eyes and saw my bones threading the mud of my grave. My eyelashes like an old maid being her most carefully concealed false: "Oh you're coming to a meet?—I bet I'll fall at the start and you wont think I can run."

"Oh dont worry I read about it in the papers, bigshot." Poking me—pinching me—"I'll be watching yerr, hey—" Then suddenly sadly getting to her girlish point, "I been missin ya."

"I been missin *you*."

"How could you!—not with Maggie Cassidy ya havent!"

"Do you know her?"

"No."

"Then how can you say that."

"Oh, I got spics. Not that I care. You know I go with Jimmy McGuire lately. Oh he's nice. Hey you'd like him. He'd make a nice friend for you. He reminds me of you. That nice kid you know, your friend from Pawtucketville . . . Lousy?—a little bit like him too. You all have the same eyes. But Jimmy's Irish, like me."

I'd stand like a precious being, listening.

"So I get along all right dont you worry I wont knit socks over *you* . . . hey did you hear me sing at the rehearsal for the Paint n Powder show? Know what I sang?"

"What?"

"Remember the night last December we went skating, that pond of yours out by Dracut and comin home in the freezing night with the moon and the frost you kissed me?"

"*Heart and Soul.*"

"That's what I'm goin to sing—" Corridors of time stretched ahead of her, songs, sadnesses, some day she'd sing for Artie Shaw, some day little gangs of colored people would gather around her microphone in Roseland Ballroom and call her the white Billy—the roommates of her hard-knock singing days would go on to be movie stars— Now at sixteen she sang *Heart and Soul* and had little affairs with bashful sentimental boys of Lowell and pushed them and said "Hey". . . .

"I'll get you back Mr. Duluoz not that I want you but you'll come crawling, that Maggie Cassidy's only trying to take you away from me to get into the act she wants to have a high school football and track all around athlete if she cant come to high school herself because she was too dumb to graduate from Junior Hi— Hey Pauline Cole is that nice!" She pushed me, then pulled me to her. "This is the last time I'll meet you under our clock." It was a big boxlike clock hanging from the wall of the school, donated by some old class when the yellowbricks were new—we'd had our first trembling meetings under it— When she sang *Heart and Soul* in the cold night snow of fields it was the melting of our hearts we thought forever— The clock was our big symbol.

"Well I'll see you *some* time."

"Not under this clock, kid."

I'd walk home alone, two hours to kill before track practice, up Moody in the wake of all the others long home and already changed for backlot yellings; Iddyboy had led the parade a long time ago with his books and eager eediboy stride ("How there boy?")—old drunks in the Silver Star and other Moody saloons watching the parade of kids— Now it was two—sad walk up through the slums, up the hill, over the bridge into the bright keen cottages and hills of Pawtucketville, perdu, perdu. Far on the Rosemont basin were the afternoon skaters in their blue; over their heads the dreams of clouds long sobbed for and lost.

I climbed the stairs to my home on the fourth floor over the Textile Lunch—nobody in, gray dismal light filtering through the curtains— In gloom I take out my Ritz crackers peanut butter and milk from the pantry with its neat news-paper lining—no housewife of the Plastic Fifties had less dust— Then, kitchen table, the light from the north win-dow, gloom views of grief-stricken birch on hills beyond the white raw roofs—my chess set and book. The book from the library; Scotch Gambit, Queen's Gambit, scholarly trea-tises on the combination of openings, the glistening chess pieces palpable to dramatize defeats—It was how I'd be-come interested in old classical-looking library books, tomes, chess critiques some of them falling apart and from the darkest shelf in the Lowell Public Library, found there by me in my overshoes at closing time—

I pondered a problem.

The green electric clock in the family since 1933 traveled its poor purring little second-hand around and around the elevated yellow numbers and dots—the paint chipping was leaving them half black, half lost—time herself rolling electrically or otherwise was eating at paints, dust slowly gathering on the hour-hand, in the works inside, in the corners of the Duluoz closets— The second-hand kisses the minute-hand sixty times an hour 24 hours a day and still we swallow in hope of life.

Maggie was far away from my thoughts, it was my rest hour—I went to the windows, looked out; looked in the mirror; sad pantomimes, faces; lay in the bed, everything unutterably gloomy, yawning, slow to come—when it would come I wouldnt know the difference. In the bleak, birds squeak. I flexed my current muscles at the mirror's flat unbending blind blare— On the radio dull booming statics half obliterated lowly songs of the time— Down on Gardner Street old Monsieur Gagnon spat and walked on— The vultures were feeding on all our chimneys, *tempus*. I stopped at the phosphorescent crucifix of Jesus and inwardly prayed to sorrow and suffer as He and so be saved. Then I walked downtown again to track, nothing gained.

The high school street was empty. A late winter afternoon pinkbleak light had fallen over it now, it had been reflected in Pauline's sad eyes— Sagging old snowbanks, a black tree, weak sister sun on the side of an old building—the keen speechless winter blue beginning to appear over eastern eve roofs as the western ones pulse to the rose of distant dayfire dimming off the low cloudbanks. The last clerk's stacking sales slips in Bon Marche's. Dusk bird bulleted to his dark-nesses. I hurried to the indoor track, where the runners drummed on boards in a dark inside tragedy of their own. Coach Joe Garrity stood bleakly clocking his new 600-yard hope who in gladiator doom pumped and pulled elastic legs to expectation. Little kids threw final meaningless socks at the farthest baskets as Joe hollered to clear the gym, echoing. I ran into the lockers to jump into my track shorts and tightfitting slipper sneakers. The gun barked the first 30-yard heat, the runners shot from tilted fingertips and dug the planks away to go. I made preliminary warm-up runs around hollow clamoring board banks. Cold, goosepimples on my arms, dust in the dumb gym.

"All right Jack," said Coach Garrity in his low calm voice, carrying across the planks like a mesmerist's, "let's see you try that new arm motion—I think that's been stoppin you for sure."

In inconceivable goofiness of my own mad mind I'd been for almost a month imitating the way Jimmy Dibbick ran, he was a distance runner, none too good, but had a way of pulling himself as he ran, hands far out fingertips stretched pointing pull-pumping like that into air reaching—a screwy style that I imitated just for fun; however in the dash, in which I was Number One man on the team beating at that time even Johnny Kazarakis who in another year beat everybody in the Eastern high schools of the United States but wasnt developed yet—the reach style was bad for my dash, I usually made 3.8 seconds in the 30, now I was retarded to 4 flat and getting beat by all kinds of kids like Louis Morin who was fifteen years old and wasnt even on the team yet just wore tennis sneakers of his own—"Run like you used to do," said Joe, "forget your arms, just run, think of your feet, *run, go,*—whatsamatter you got woman troubles?" he grinned cheerlessly but with a wise humor gained from the fact that he lived no life of recognition and ease, the best track coach in Massachusetts he nevertheless worked at some desk job all day in City Hall and had a handful of responsibility small-paying him. "Come on Jack, run— you're my only sprinter this year."

In the low hurdles among these kids I couldn't beat, I flew ahead; in Boston Garden roaring with all the high schools of New England I ran meek thirds behind longlegged ghosts two of them from Newton and everybody from Brockton, from Peabody, Framingham, Quincy and Weymouth, from Somerville, Waltham, Malden, Lynn, Chelsea—from the bird, endless.

I got down on the line with a group of others, spat on the planks, dug my sneakers in, balanced, trembling, shot off expecting Joe's gun and had to walk back sheepish— Now he held the gun up, we teetered, wondered, aimed eyes down the boards—BRAM! Off we go, I kick myself out with my right arm I let the arms pump themselves crosswise over my chest and run headlong falling for the line furious. They clock me in 3.7, I win by two yards blamming into the big mat against the finish line wall, glad.

"There," says Joe, "didja ever hit 3.7 before?"

"No!"

"They musta made a mistake timing. But you got it now, pump those arms natural. All right! Hurdles!"

We put up the low hurdles, wood, some of them need new nails. We line up, blam, off we go—I've got every step figured, by the time we reach the first hurdle my left leg is ready to go over, I do so, slapping it down fast on the other side, *stepping,* the right leg horizontal folded to fly, arms swinging the move. Between first and second hurdles I jump and sprint and stretch and bound the necessary five strides and go over again, this time alone, the others are behind—I go down to the tape 35 yards two hurdles in 4.7.

The 300 was my nemesis; it meant running as fast as I could for almost a minute— 39 seconds or so—a terrible grueling grind of legs, bone, muscle, wind and flailing poor legs lungs—it also meant gnashing smashing bumps with the others around the first turn, sometimes a guy'd go flying off the bank flat on his ass on the floor full of slivers it was so rough, foaming-at-the-mouth Emil Ladeau used to give me huge whomps on the first bank and especially the last when panting sickfaced we stretched that last twenty yards to dic at the tape— I'd beat Emil but I told Joe I didnt want to run that thing any more—he conceded to my sensitivity but insisted I run in the 300-yard relays (with Melis, Mickey McNeal, Kazarakis)—we had the best 300-yard relay in the state and even beat St. John's Prep older collegians in the Boston finals— So every afternoon I'd have to run the bloody 300 usually in a relay race, just to the clock, against another little kid twenty yards behind me and no footballing on the banks—Sometimes girls would come and watch their boyfriends in track practice, Maggie'd never have dreamed it she was so gloomy and lost in herself.

Pretty soon it'll be time for the 600—the 1000—broad jump—shot put—then home we go—for supper—then the phone—and Maggie's voice. Aftersupper Lowell talking to me—"Can I come tonight?"

"I told you Wednesday."

"That's too far away—"

"You're *cray*-zee."

—as lonely glooms fall enfolding all the warm organic rooftops of living Lowell—

14

After the last six o'clock shot put, the ball in the fingers delicately against the neck cradled, the kick, the hop, the twist of waist, the push up and out of the ball high and far—this was fun—I'd go in to showers and re-dress to again for the third time in my busy crazy high day stride Moody Street determined, young, and wild—a mile home. In winter darkness, the Baghdad Arabian keenblue deepness of the piercing lovely January winter's dusk—it used to tear my heart out, one stabbing soft star was in the middle of the magicalest blue, throbbing like love—I saw Maggie's black hair in this night—In the shelves of Orion her eye shades, borrowed, gleamed a dark and proud vellum somber power brooding rich bracelets of the moon rose from our snow, and surrounded the mystery. Smoke whipped from clean chimneys of Lowell. Now at Worthen, Prince and other old milltown streets as my feet shot me past I saw the redbrick faded into something cold and rose—unspeeched—throat-choking— My father's ghost in a gray felt hat walked the dirty snows—*"Ti Jean t'en rappelle quand Papa travailla pour le Citizen?—pour L'Etoile?"* (Remember when your father worked for the Citizen, for the Star?)—I hoped my father'd be home that week end—I wished he could give me advice for Maggie—and in the grim mill alleys of ink blue and lost solstice rose he moseyed shades aside moaning my name, big, shadowy, lost—I shot past the Library now brown-windowed for scholars of the winter eve, the reading room bums, the children's library roundshelved fairytaled and sweet—the profound bloodred bricks of the old Episcopalian church, the brown lawn, the jag of snow, the sign announcing speeches— Then the Royal Theater, crazy movies, Ken Maynard, Bob Steele, the French Canadian tenements seen up side streets, the gay winter North—remnant Christmas bulbs— Then Ah the bridge, the sigh of waters, the soothe big roar low wind coming in from Chelmsford, from Dracut, from the north—the orange iron implacable dusk skies pinpointing the steeples, and roofs in a still gloom, the iron arbrous brows of old hills far off—everything engraved and glided upon the eve and that frozen still. . . . My shoes clomped the bridge boards. My nose snuffled. A long and tiresome day and far from finished.

I passed the Textile Lunch windows, saw the bent fisty eaters through steam panes, and turned smartly into my gloomy rank doorway—736 Moody Street—dank—up four flights in eternity. In.

"Bon, Ti Jean est arrivez!" my mother said.

"Bon!" my father said, he was home, there was his face peeking around the kitchen door with a big Oriental grin— At table, my mother's loaded it with food, steamings, goodies, he's been feasting for an hour—I rush up and kiss his sad rough face.

"By golly I got here just in time to see you run against Worcester Satty night!"

"That's right!"

"Now you'll have to show me what you can do boy!"

"I will!"

"Eat! Look at the spread your mother's got here."

"I'll wash!"

"Hurry!"

I wash, come in combed, start eating; Pa's peeling his apple with his scout knife. "Well, I'm all through at Andover— Might as well tell you now— They're laying off, their rush season— I can try Rolfe's here in Lowell—"

"*Ben oui!*" my mother in French. "It's much better you stay home!"—her tearful way of arguing and always her arguments are sweet.

"Okay, okay," laughing—"I'll try my best. Well my little tyke, how are you my boy! Say, maybe I can get a job at McGuire's where Nin is— Say, what's this I hear about you going around mooning over some little Irish girl— Bet she's a beauty, hey? Well You're too young for that. Ha ha ha. Well dammit, I'm home again."

"Home *agin!*"—Ma.

"Hey Pa I'll play you a game of football with the board— Whattaya say?"

"I was thinking of going down to the Club and bowling a few strings—"

"Well okay, *one* game—and I'll go bowl you a game!"

"It's a deal!"—laughing, coughing on his cigar, bending quickly with huge red-faced excitement to scratch his ankle.

"Okay," says my mother proud and flushed and lala'ing to have her old man home again, "you do that and I'll clear the table right away and make a nice fresh pot of coffee— aye?"

And in from the joyous cold night of the North come Lousy, Billy Artaud and Iddyboy, there are big jokes and laughs, and we choose sides, toss coins, pick teams and play a game. In the windows is slow frost, the lamplights below are in a cold and lonely black but quick figures breathing fog pass swiftly beneath them to definite eager destinations—

Not knowing that I dont deserve life without praising God I sneak off from the kitchen for a quick quiet phone call in the dark parlor—calling Maggie— Her little sister Janie answers. Maggie comes to the phone with a simple tired-sounding "Hi."

"Hi—Wednesday night I'm comin over huh?"

"I *told* you."

"What are you doing tonight?"

"Oh nothing. I'm bored to tears. Roy and his girl are pl—that are getting married in August are playin cards. My father just left to go to work, they gave him a short call, you shoulda seen him run out the door—he forgot his railroad watch on the dresser— He'll be hoppin mad!"

"*My* father's home."

"I'd like to meet your father sometime."

"You'll like him."

"What'd you do all day?—not that it's important . . ."

"I do the same thing every day—walk, school, walk back for a nap, walk back for track—"

"Spendin all your time talking to Pauline Cole under the clock?"

"Sometimes." I didnt hide it or anything. "Doesnt matter."

"Just friends, huh?"

In the way she said "huh?" I saw her whole body and lips and wanted to clup her a mad one she'd never forget.

"Hey—"

"What?"

"If you're bored to tears I'll come over tonight!"

"Okay."

"But I havent got time" (surprised I was). "But I will."

"No. You said you didnt have time."

"Yes I do."

"You said you dint."

"See you in an hour."

"Never mind . . ."

"Hah? I'll be right over. Hey."

To my father and friends riotously laughing in the kitchen: "Hey, I think I'll go see . . . Maggie Cassidy . . . that girl I know . . . she . . . we just . . . have to help her brother with his homework—"

"Aw," said my father looking up with frank stunned eyes, very blue eyes, "it's my first night home, you said we'd go bowling— We'll choose sides with the boys—"

"Zeet? Me and your Pop against you and Iddyboy!" cried Lousy in eager glee squeezing himself, then, to me, low, looking over his shoulder, for the benefit of everybody, "Maggie Cassidy that was? Ah Zagg you Babe that aint right cheatin on Pauline Cole! Hee hee! Hey Mister Duluoz we call Jack Zagg-you-Babe now— Hear that," grabbing me by the neck and making a frown, "now he's cheatin on Moe Cole— Let's drown him in the water, throw him in the snow—"

"Eeedyboy!" echoed Iddyboy with shining eyes showing me his huge fist. "I going to fix you Jack and knock you through the fence!" We made wrestler faces at each other.

Impatiently my mother: "Stay here, stay home Jean—"

Rubbing his hands wirily Billy Artaud: "He knows when

he's beat! Doesnt wanta accept that challenge bowling—
Let him go!" he finally yelled above all the others trium-
phantly as a commotion in the kitchen rose making little
spiderwebs of the corner ceiling wave. "That leaves four of
us, *we'll* have a bowling party—and Missiz Duluoz can keep
the score!"

This raised roars of noise and laughing. I had a chance
to go. All in life, prime, youngjoy days, riches of sixteen,
I sneaked off to the lazy unresponsive girl three miles across
town by the tragic-flowing dark sad Concord.

I took the bus—at the last minute avoiding my father's
eyes—telling myself "I'll see him tomorrow for gosh
sakes—" Ride the bus, guiltish, depressed, looking down,
always the dross and dirty loss spine ribbing down life's
poor gold and it so short and sweet.

It was a Monday night.

15

From Pawtucketville to South Lowell the route by bus en-
compassed the city—down Moody, to Kearney Square below
the high school, the fleet of buses, the people huddled
waiting against doorfronts of soda parlors, 5 & 10s, drug-
stores— The sad traffic crunching in from winter, out to
winter— The bleak blue raw feel of the wind from the woods
cityfying by the few sad lights— There I changed to the
South Lowell bus— It would show up always catching at
my throat—the mere name of it as the busdriver'd rolled
it in the window enough to make my heart beat—I'd look

at other people's faces to see if they saw the magic— The
ride itself grew grimmer— From the Square out up Central,
to Back Central, to the outlying dark long streets of the
town where dim frost sits the night by howling-wind garbage
pails in cold moonlight— Out along the Concord where
factories enlisted its famous flow—out beyond even them—
to a dark highway where Massachusetts Street under a brown
dumb streetlamp spoked in, small, mean, old, full of my
love and the name of it— There I'd get off the bus, among
trees, by the river, and dodge the mudholes, seven cottages
down on the right to her rambling old unfenced brown-
windowed house overtopped by clacking skeletal trees of the
sudden from-Boston sea winds blown over wilderness, rail-
yards and hoar— Each house meant my heart beat faster as
it passed my rapid step. Her actual house, the actual light
that actually upon her was bestowing and around her bath-
ing, mote by mote made rare gold, dear magic, was the
commotion hysterical light of wonder— Shadows on her
porch? Voices in the street, in the yard? Not a sound, but
the dull Victorian wind moaning New England by the river
in the winter night—I'd stop in the street outside her house.
One figure within—her mother—gloomy pawing in the
kitchen, turning sadly in life, putting away her sweet dishes
that some day they'd pack away with guilt and sorrow and
say "I never knew, I never knew!"— The dumb, the spittling
mankind crawing in his groin to make nothing.

Where is Maggie? O wind, songs have ye in her name?
Plucked her did ye from midnight blasted millyard winds
and made her renown ring in stone and brick and ice? Hard
implacable bridges of iron cross her milk of brows? God
bent from his steel arc welded her a hammer of honey and
of balm?

The rutted mud of hardrock Time . . . was it wetted, springified, greened, blossomied for me to grow in nameless bloodied lutey naming of her? Wood on cold trees would her coffin bare? Keys of stone rippled by icy streaks would ope my needy warm interiors and make her eat the soft sin of me? No iron bend or melt to make my rocky travail ease—I was all alone, my fate was banged behind an iron door, I'd come like butter looking for Hot Metals to love, I'd raise my feeble orgone bones and let them be rove and split the half and goop the big sad eyes to see it and say nothing. The laurel wreath is made of iron, and thorns of nails; acid spit, impossible mountains, and incomprehensible satires of blank humanity—congeal, cark, sink and seal my blood—

"*There* you are. What are you standing out in the road for? What'd ya come for?"

"Didnt we decide on the phone?"

"Oh . . . maybe you did."

This made me mad and I didnt say anything; now she was in her element.

"What are you so quiet about, Jacky Boy?"

"You oughta know. Dont call me Jacky Boy. Why were you on the porch. I didnt see you!"

"I saw you comin down the street. All the way from the bus."

"It's cold out."

"I'm wrapped in my coat snug. Come on in with me."

"In your coat."

Laugh. "Silly. In the house. Nobody home. My mother's goin to Mrs. O'Garra tonight to hear the Firestone Hour, some singer."

"I though you didnt want me to come. Now you're glad."

"How do y'know?"

"When you squeeze my hand like that."

"Sometimes you get me. Sometimes I cant stand how I love you."

"Hah?"

"Jacky!" And she was on me, all of her, thrown socko into me all huddled to my frame, clung, kissing me wild and deep and hot—desperate—it would never have happened on a regular Wednesday or Saturday night planned date— I closed my eyes, felt faint, lost, heartbroken, salt-sunk drowned.

In my ear, warm, hot lips, whisperings, "I love you Jacky. Why do you make me so mad! Oh you make me so mad! Oh I love you so! Oh I wanta kiss you! Oh you damn fool I want you to take me. I'm yours dont you know?—all, all yours—you're a fool Jacky—Oh poor Jacky— Oh kiss me— *hard*—save me!—I need you!" Not even inside the house yet. In there, by the hissing radiator, on the couch, we practically did everything there is to do but I never touched her in the prime focal points, previous trembling places, breasts, the moist star of her thighs, even her legs—I avoided it to please her— Her body was like fire, packed soft and round in a soft dress, young—firm-soft, rich—a big mistake—her lips burned all over my face. We didnt know where we were, what to do. And dark moved the Concord in the winter night.

"I'm glad I came!" I told myself jubilantly. "If Pa could see this or feel this he'd *know* now, he wouldnt be disappointed—Lousy too!—Ma!—I'm gonna marry Maggie, I'm gonna tell Ma!"—I pulled her yielding yearning waist, it

popped her pelvis bone right into mine, I gritted my teeth
in the memory of the future—

"I'm goin to the Rex Saturday night," she said, pouting
in the dark as I licked her lower lip with my fingertip then
threw my hand on the floor off the couch and she was
suddenly stroking my profile. ("You look like you're cut
out of rock.")

"I'll meet you there."

"I wish you were older."

"Why?"

"You'd know more what to do with me—"

"If—"

"No! You dont know how. I love you too much. What's
the use? Oh hell—I love you so! But I hate you! Oh go
home!! Kiss me! Lie on top of me, crush me—" Kisses—
"Jacky I wrote you a big note today and tore it up—too
much in it—"

"I read the one—"

"I finally sent that one—I wanted you to marry me in
my first note— I know you're too young, I'm robbing the
high school cradle."

"Ah—"

"You have no trade—You have a career ahead of
you—"

"No no—"

"—be a brakeman on the railroad, we'll live in a little
house by the tracks, play the 920 Club, have babies— I'll
paint my kitchen chairs red—I'll paint the walls of our
bedroom deep dark green or sumpin—I'll kiss you to wake
up in the morning—"

"Oh Maggie that's what I want!" (Maggie Cassidy? I thought wildly. Maggie Cassidy! Maggie Cassidy!)

"No!" Slapping me on the face—pushing it—angry, pouting, rolling away, sitting up to roundabout her dress again straight. "Hear me? No!"

I'd wrestle her to the bottom of the dark couch retwisting her dresses slips belts and girdly toot pots both of us panting, sweating, burning— Hours passed, it was midnight, my day was not done— Reverently my hair was falling in her eyes.

"Oh Jack it's too late."

"I dont wanta go."

"You gotta go."

"Ah okay."

"I dont want you to go—I love you to kiss me—— Dont let that Pauline Cole steal you away from me. Dont make faces like that I'll get up and walk away—Jacky—I love you I love I love you—" She kept saying it into my mouth—through my teeth, bit my lip— There were tears of joy in her eyes, on her cheeks; her warm body smelled ambrosial brew in the profound struggle we waged sinking in pillows, bliss, madness, night—hours on end—

"You better go home, dear— You gotta go to school tomorrer— You'll never get up."

"Okay Maggie."

"Say you love me when you wake up in the morning, to yourself—"

"How could I . . . otherwise . . . do . . ."

"Call me tomorrer night—come Friday—"

"W—"

"I mean Wednesday! Kiss me! Hold me! I love you I always will and no one else ever ever—I never was so much in love—never again—you damn Canook you—"

"I cant leave."

"Leave. Dont let nobody tell you nothin about me."

"Nobody *does!*"

"If they do . . .

"If they did I wouldnt lissen—Maggie that house by the railroad tracks, the red chairs . . . I . . . I . . . cant—dont want to do anything else with anybody else—ever— I'll tell—I'll—we'll— Ah Maggie."

She'd cradle my broken head in her all-healing lap that beat like a heart; my eyes hot would feel the soothe fingertips of cool, the joy, the stroke and barely-touch, the feminine sweet lost bemused inward-biting far-thinking deep earth river-mad April caress—the brooding river in her unfathomable springtime thoughts— The dark flowing enriched silty heart— Irish as peat, dark as Kilkenny night, sorcerous as elf, red-lipped as red-rubied morn on the Irish Sea on the east coast as I have seen it, promising as the thatched roofs and green swards there bringing tears to my eyes to be an Irishman too and lost and sunk inside her forever—her brother, husband, lover, raper, owner, friend, father, son, grabber, kisser, keener, swain, sneaker-upper, sleeper-with, feeler, railroad brakeman in red house of red babycribs and the joyous wash Saturday morning in the glad ragged yard—

I walked home in the dead of Lowell night—three miles, no buses—the dark ground, roads, cemeteries, streets, construction ditches, millyards— The billion winter stars hugeing overhead like frozen beads frozen suns all packed and inter-allied in one rich united universe of showery light, beating, beating, like great hearts in the non-understandable bowl void black.

To which nevertheless I offered up all my songs and longwalk sighs and sayings, as if they could hear me, know, care.

16

Walking home the last mile as all Lowell snored I imagined myself a far traveler looking for a place to sleep—"Well, pretty soon I'll have to turn in at one of these houses and go to bed, I cant go on much further"—and I'd clack along on the crunchy snows and grits of sidewalks, past moonlight-whitened wash-hung courts of Moody tenements, past taxi-cab stands with a one red light in night, past hamburger lunchcarts with inscrutable shadows munching within in smoke and heat obscured by vapors of the written glass— For the sixth time in the day I'd come to the great bridge a hundred feet over the river and see down there the tiny milky rivulets of icy Time gurgling in the rockjags, the reflection of starry paradises in profound black pools, the squawk of strange birds eating mist— Clack went the trees of Riverside as I hushed and nose pinched stumbled on home—"I guess I'll have to turn in this house here—no, the next one— Well, I guess I'll take the fifth one— That's what— I'll just walk in and go right to sleep cause the whole world has invited me to sleep in their house so it doesnt matter what house I go to—"

And I'd turn into 736 Moody and go upstairs and go in the door left unlocked by my family and hear my father's profound snore in their bedroom and go to my spectral room with the big bed and *Jack Jump Over the Candlestick* on the wall and say to myself, "Well, this is a nice place, I think I'll sleep in this bed, these people seem nice"—and with strange self-induced whacky but deeply comfortable wonder I'd undress and go to bed and look in the dark at darkness— and fall asleep in the lap of warm life there.

And in the morning my eyes wouldnt unglue, at breakfast I'd decide to play hooky again, go to Vinny's and take a nap. All the winter world goldened and shined white—

17

Vinny's was the big scene of suicide hookies, we'd have wild parties all day screaming—"Come on G.J., play hooky with me today" I'd say at the corner of Riverside and he would and so would Lousy.

"Zagg, you cant talk me out of it!"

Sometimes Scotty'd come, and one time Skunk, and finally with Vinny we began passing up the sprawlings and eatings and yelling with the radio in his house when sometimes we'd have big fights and knock down curtains and it was a job to clean up for the millworking mother—talking about girls instead, listening to Harry James, writing screwy letters to everybody— We began hitting the Club de Paisan poolhall which was a shack in the Aiken Street dump behind the tenements of Little Canada— Here an old ninety-year-old man with perfect bowed legs stood by a potbelly stove with an old French Canadian red Indian handkerchief to his nose and watched us (red eyes) tossing nickles on the torn pool table for who gets the break. The wind howled and moaned at the hinges; it was huge snow storms we'd pass there, the great gale of snows would whip past the plate-glass windows in one horizontal wild line from Canada coming, from the Sweeps of Baffin Bay—and we were alone in the Club. Nobody else would think of going to such a beat old shack—it was for local winos of Cheever and the river bank probably to in the evening come in with stinking pipes humble old guys spitting in planks—*Le Club de Paisan*—Club of Oldfashioned Peasants—Vinny screeched and danced around on the loose old boards through which the blizzard cold seeped but the stove held out, the old man stoked it, stocked it and kicked it, he knew how to make a fire like he knew how to eat.

"Hey Pop!" they'd call him. Scotty and I, respectful, called him *"L'Père"* and he always knew the weather. For years of our lost numb childhoods he'd been sitting in wooden tenement lazy afternoon doorways of Moody and Lilley on the Lowell Fellaheen French Day—babies had yodeled, his old ears had heard generations come and go, croaking. Every game we played we threw him a nickel. "Okay my break Scott!"

"Ah go on—that nickel was leaning—"

"Kick him, you babe, kick him—"

They overturn a chair and a bucket, the old man doesnt even bat an eyelash. Our glory's all wild in the gray storm of shacks and dumps outside—our histories weighted down in the middle with unbelievable freights of moment by moment drowsy life hours that our mothers have carried on their eyelashes since our inceptions from their aprons and the first heroic events of infancy. Beautiful Vinny's glory lay in his eyes, health, screams. "If you guys dont stop shaking that table the way you have been doing I'll be ga-dammed for about ask Mouse a halfa fuggen hour I'm gonna get my boxing gloves and my rubbers and load em full of bolts and screws and swing from the floor as hard as I can with all my weight and kick myself in the ass if I dont brain both of you flat on the floor, like cows' shining azzholes, dead." And we saw that he was going to do it if we didn't stop shaking the table. Scotty didnt even have to mention anything, we saw flashes of murder in his somber thunder-storm eyes. Lousy was a streak of terrible lightning if some-thing should suddenly happen, you wouldn't see him and the air wouldnt split—suave litotical transsubstantiations of a thrush—I was a self-satisfied dreaming bull supine on the bench or lost in thought shooting at the table—eying my Coca-Cola. G.J.'s Greekly rage was buried in his kind politeness and in his humor and goodness:—he'd have slit the Sicilian from top to bottom in other Mediterraneas, showing but yellow of his eyes.

18

Meanwhile my father was walking along the redbrick walls of commercial Lowell, in the blizzard, looking for a job. He walked into the dark dank printing plant—Rolfe's.

"Say Jim, how've you been, I want to know if you've got

an opening here for a good linotyper with years of experience—"

"Emil! Great Jesus, Emil!"

"Hi Jim."

"Where in the hell you been? Hey Charley, look, Emil— Crazy Emil—what you been doin in Andover I hear—"

"Oh yeah, working well framblin and dandlin around looking for something to do— Still got a wife, y'know, and two kids, Jacky's in high school running with the track team this winter— Say, I see old Cogan aint here any more."

"No, he died last April."

"Ya dont say-y . . . Well I'll be dammed. *He* was over seventy wasnt he?"—both in dark satisfied agreement— "Well old poor Cogan many's the time I saw him pushing and rushing that old wagon around, you'd think a man could work his life out just workin—"

"That's right, Emil—" Quick muse—"In fact Emil—" (and now the job's sewed up because Rolfe hasnt got anybody else he knows in New England he'd rather have right now than Emil Duluoz and with the rush season on) "—last Saturday night I worked for the *Tele*, they called me up 'bout six o'clock, their regular man was sick and layin off so I said 'Okay' and I went up and boy I melted lead and turned out more galleys a ten-ton truck and it was about six o'clock in the morning when I finished and the back of my neck, and my feet numb from sitting all night—"

"I know Jim— Only last week it was old fartface come up to me and wanted me to go to a show with him then a game over to Bill Wilson's room in the hotel down there see this is all in Lawrence he'd drive me from Andover we had— Oh we saw a lot of nice gals dancing there ya know, hoopsidoo, that Gem Club, on Hollis Street, we had a few beers, I said to Bill 'I gotta finish this copy if you dont mind Bill looks to me like it'll take me to well nigh near midnight'—"

Meanwhile a kid is waiting with papers in his hand for the two old bucks the boss and the big fat man to stop talking but they wont—

Emil, a half-hour later, steps out into the snow, coughs hugely, cigar-a-mouth, and minces off like Babe Ruth or W. C. Fields with the same pout and little short steps but also with a leering pathetical grin looking at everybody and digging all the streets of Lowell with his eyes.

"Oh for krissakes, there goes that old Charley McConnell he's had that damn Model-T Ford ever since I got mine in 1929 and that was at Lakeview for the picnic there and even then he'd have that same look of pitiful defeat in his face, still and all he's made out all right from what I hear— That job in City Hall pays him fairly well and certainly hasnt killed him and he's got a house in the Highlands— *I* never had anything against McConnell"—(scoffing with himself, coughing)—"Well it's all in the way the rain barrel rolls over I guess, they'll spill em out one by one to the hole in the ground out by Edson's Cemetery and we'll take no more trips to Boston that way . . . The years, the years, that I've seen . . . eat . . . the faces . . . of respectable . . . and . . . disrespectable people . . . in this town . . . they cant . . . tell me . . . I don't know who's heir to Heaven, hell, riches, gold and all the immense uncounted cash registers and poorpot pissplots of every grave from here to the Roman diosee and back by golly I've seen and heard it all. When they put me away they better not spend too much money, *I* wont appreciate it from my bed of clay— *They'd* better learn that now. Ha ha ha ha! What a town when you come to think of it—*Lowell*—" He heaved a sigh. "Well it's where my little woman hung her curtains, I guess. The sucker was in the kitchen sittin by the radio, name of Emil. I guess the old lady had it coming to her, to inherit a beast and at the same time I guess she didnt do too bad with the pieces of—grass—I was able to lay around her picnic. My wife Angry— Okay. *God*, tell me if anything goes wrong and you dont want me to go on that way. I'm just tryna please. If I cant please You, and the world, and Ti Jean too, then I cant please the lion and the angel and the lamb all at the same time neither. Thank you God, and get those Democrats outa there before this country goes to hell!"

By now he'd be talking out loud to himself and cutting through the snow head bent, teeth gricked to the sleet, hatbrim down, coat whitening, in the wonderful mysterious hours of an ordinary day in ordinary life in ordinary cold blue life.

Rushing from the Club de Paisan at one o'clock, the day's school over, with G.J. and the gang striding, I'd run into my father rounding the corner of the Moody Street Bridge right in the howl-shroud of the gale itself blowing over the city's bridges, and on across the snowy boards we'd bowl home, the gang in front, Pa and I in back, jawing and jabbering.

"Goin to track practice at four—"

"I'll be there for the opening scene Satty night— Say, how 'bout goin down together?"

"Sure. We'll ride down with Louis Morin and Emil Ladeau in the bus—"

"Ah Ti Jean, I'm glad ta see ya making good on the track team, it makes my old heart proud by golly. I got a job

at Rolfe's this afternoon—looks like I'll be around awhile—
Old Gloomy Puss— well I'll have my upsets, but pay no
attention to me. I'll be ranting about the government, about
the way America has changed since I was a boy. Dont pay
it any attention, kiddo—but maybe when you grow older
you'll understand my feelings."

"Yeah, Pa."

"Whattaya think of that—ha ha ha—"

"Say Pa!"

"What kiddo?" turning to me eagerly with laughter and
shining eyes.

"Did you know who finally beat that Whitney colt down
in Florida."

"Yeah, I know, I had one-fifty across the board on him
in the club, the bum— Yeah, k—Ti J—Jack—"(stam-
mering to find my name) "yeah kiddo," seriously, far away,
broodingly squeezing my arm, realizing I'm just a child.
"Yeah me boy—yeah sonny—my kid—"and in his eyes a
mysterious mist, dense with tears, springing from the secret
earth of his being and always dark, unknown, come of itself,
like there is no reason for a river.

"It'll come, Jack—" and in his countenance you saw he
meant just death— "What'll be with it? Maybe you gotta
know a lot of people in Heaven to make life succeed. It'll
come. You dont have to know a soul to know what I know—
to expect what I'm expecting—to feel yourself alive and
dying in your chest every minute of the livelong day—
When you're young you wanta cry, when you're old you
wanta die. But that's too deep for you now, *Ti mon Pousse*"
(Little My Thumb).

19

Wednesday night came slowly.

"Sit here, by me."

It's Maggie, solemn, her legs crossed, hands folded on her lap, on the couch, in the parlor, fullblast overhead lights, her cousin is going to show us how his magic trick works. It's some kid thing out of a kit book, I'm bored (like by television), but Maggie is dead serious and skeptical and watching every move Tommy makes because as she says, "He's such a devil, you gotta watch him, he'll play the *meanest* tricks and tease ya, he's almost a sneak"— Tommy the handsome popular boy cousin that all the Cassidy girls love and look up to and roar and laugh in parlors and kitchens as he performs and does headstands of activity, a good kid, shining eyes, his hair falling in them, full of glee, the little kids alrady sent to bed are peeking from the top of the stairs where the wallpaper is lit a dim rose by the nightlamp— So I watch Maggie watch Tommy—out of the corner of my eye. Tonight she's more beautiful than ever, she has a little white rose or flower of some kind in her hair, to the left, her hair comes down on both sides of her brow almost over the corners of her eyes, her lips pursed (chewing gum) to watch and doubt. She has a lace collar, very neat, she went to church that afternoon and to Mrs. O'Garra down Chelmsford Road to get that cakemix for the party. She has a crucifix on her dress breast; lace ends on her short sleeves; little bracelets on both wrists; hands crossed, sweet white fingers I eye with immortal longing to hold in mine and have to wait—fingers I know well, cold slightly, moving, nudging a little as she laughs but primly stay folded in her hands—her legs crossed show sweet knees, no stockings, the well-formed calf below, the hint of snowy legs, the little dress pathetically draping off this ladylike arrangement of herself. Her hair hangs, black and heavy, soft, smooth, curly, to her back—the white flesh and the sullen unbelieving river eyes more beautiful than the eyes of all the sun-eyed blondes of MGM, Scandinavia and the western world— The milk of the brow, the pear of the face, the solid silky proud erect neck of the young girl—I take her all in for the hundredth time that night.

"Oh *Tommy*—stop fooling with it and let's see the trick!" she cries, turning exasperated away.

"Yes!" cries Bessy Jones, and little Janie and the mother Cassidy seated with us partly reading the paper and Maggie's brother Roy the railroad brakeman like his father is standing in the door with a loose smile, eating a sandwich, his hands black-in with grime of his job, his teeth pearly white, in his dark eyes the some Irish contemptuous disbelief of tricks and games and yet the same greedy avid interest—so that he too yelled out now "Ah Tom you bull thrower do that red handkerchief one again— This one's bull, I seen what you did—"

I smile to show that I'm interested in everything but in the brown wallpapered parlor of eternity my heart only beats for her so sweet just a pace away, my life.

"Hey," turning to me the drowning devouring scrutinizing coverage of black merry sad eyes in their incredible snow cameo skin, "you didnt see him that time, you were lookin at the floor."

"Lookin at the floor?" laughed the comedian magician. "All my work is going for fraught! Watch this Roy!"

"Yeah."

"Do it!" screeched Maggie.

"Maggie!"—the mother—"dont yell so! Ye'll have the neighbors think we drown cats in here, Luke McGarrity and his upsidedown clay pipe if ever I saw him in this picture in this magazine!" and her matronly big body shaking slowly with laughter. In my bleakness I even accepted the fact Maggie might look like her mother some day, big and fat.

"Come on, you J-a-c-k! You missed it again! Let me show you a trick I did last year for Bessy's uncle the night he walked out and tripped on the milk can and Ma's chair that was painted was on the porch and he fell on it and broke it— Lookout!" jumping up from the pose so sweet, to run around the room chasing her cousin, like a little eager flushed girl now, a minute ago a portrait of a lady in a cameo ring, with crucifix.

Later—on the porch alone—before going in—necking furiously because Bessy was still inside giggling with Jimmy McFee— "Oh go home! Go home! Go home!" she pulled at me angrily as I held her laughing in my arms, I'd said something that irritated her—her flashes of indignation, poutings, rougeings in nature, of cheek, the lovely frown and forewarning and return of her white smile—

"Okay I'll go"—but I come back again, start kidding her and kissing her again, overdo everything, and she gets mad again but really mad this time and that makes me sore and we pout and look away—"I'll see ya Monday afternoon, ah?"

"Hmf—" (she'd wanted me to see her Saturday night but that was the track meet night and I'd end up at midnight with my Pop in some soda fountain downtown talking with all the guys about the meet and who the high scorer was—

big eager-teeth guys with newspapers in cafeterias of the
night, Lowell style, a small city well famed for its great
cafeteria and soda-fountain devotees, as evidenced and pub-
licized extensively in the local paper in a column written
by James G. Santos who'd once worked with my Pa in small
newspaper days and was a distant cousin also to G.J.)—
Maggie would have to reason me out of a Rex Ballroom
dance on that night because not I'd be weary from the races
and overly hung-up with my father but I'd be so late to the
dance it wouldnt be worth the price of admission—not
wanting Maggie to think me a cheapskate I never mention
this—and she thinks I really want to sneak out with Pauline
Cole like a real smalltown hotshot maybe in fast cars at 1
A.M. on black tar tragedies out by Lakeview—"Dont come
then."

"It's better—I'll be 11:30 before I'm even out of the
showers," I plead.

"Bloodworth'll be at the Rex."

"Charley?" I was surprised; Charley was an old football
team friend who'd only met Maggie accidentally when I ran
into him accidentally at a dance one night— His open
interest in Maggie I didnt take seriously, she always flirted—
He in fact discussed her with me seriously.

"M.C.," he called her, initials, "old M.C.'ll be mad if
she knows you didnt show up to track practice the other
day, son, Bill—" (he also called me Bill, for Bill Demon)—
"us demons and them demonettes is got to stick together"—
some talk out of a Popeye cartoon running every night in
the Lowell *Sun* the local paper "so us demons is got to watch
out for the demonettes, M.C. Number Two" (he took such
a vast interest in my affairs he called Moe Cole M.C. Number

Two, and the initials fitted—all in the joy mornings of high
school life here's these wild complexities happening our
minds exploding)—

"It's okay Charley—you take over M.C. Number Two
and I'll meet you in Heaven." We joked about it; once he
took me to his house and showed me his scrapbook full of
pasted pictures of baseball stars of 1920's and 1930's with
incredibly old stars whose bones are long interred in crumbling files in the archives of red sun sinking in the Ninth
Inning with Nobody On— Seriously, with bleak youngkid
dis-knowledge of the incredible ruin of the years and the
death they have wreaked on the flesh and jawbones of men
including baseball stars, he'd in his scrapbook of 1939 stick
the old wan visages of Cincinnati left fielders of the Depression years who just made it from the minors (JOHNNY
DEERING wasnt even a jockey yet), names of old players,
Dusty Cooke, Whitey Moore—Kiki Cuyler—Johnny Coo-
ney—Heinie Manush—lost forever the still figure in right
center with a tanned taut expression on solid legs waiting
for the crack of the bat as a little shrill creamy whistle splits
the atmosphere stadium hush, the bottomless thapping dull
plop of the ball in the catcher's mitt and right after it the
umpire's *ump-euoo*! And the guy that's been ya-yagging all
afternoon from third base box again says "Ya-yag!" with
strange forlorn little voice through cupped hands at the
batter with bat back tense and an airplane drones—which
I'd see and hear all sadly white-flour pasted in his book of
books on his parlor rug in the Highlands. Then we'd rush
over to Timmy Clancy's house to play Benny Goodman Artie
Shaw records, Clancy'd be the catcher on the spring Lowell
High School team and in time President of the United States

the way he was politicking the school, the city, had once been Junior Day Mayor of Lowell with big picture of him officiating at a desk, his a name I'd seen with awe in Lowell High School baseball boxscores the year before—all of which was shouting talk in record-playing afternoons and new fresh life excitements of the inevitable High School Springtime in America. I liked Bloodworth and in the spring we were going to play outfield together on that Lowell team, he whose name for years (*Bloodworth*) had mystified me when I saw it in Lowell High and Lowell Twi League boxscore— admired him and he was going to show me how to hit a curve when the first green bedsprings of turf began to show among the brown scrags of Lowell Highlands grass (out in left with the football lines still showing in)— I liked the way he'd say "Oh that guy can *belt* em a mile, seventeen triples last year Bill! And wait'll you see Taffy Truman pitch *this* year, he's been great but this is his year!" Everything was opening up, Taffy Truman was a stylish southpaw with a gape in his front teeth and an incredibly suave draped body, just the way a pitcher should look, Lefty Grove in a loose suit—and he was good, Boston in the National League was after him— Bloodworth's interest in Maggie seemed to roll over my head and not serious because I wouldnt notice them and I trusted her to love only me. So she was going to meet him Saturday while I ran in track.

"I'll take M.C. Number One home and take good care of her," Charley'd wink at me—he had a faintly hooked nose and a funny pointed jaw and also separations in the front teeth and a glamorous looseness that made him sensationally look like a center fielder, Bloodworth cf, leadoff man—fast, he cracked electrifying singles into right with one arc-y swing of his southpaw bat . . . made of some paler ash than the others. Ash was the color of his hair too.

"Okay Bill, I'll take M.C. Number One home and see no guys follow her in cars and try to pick her up," and here'd turn away snuffing into himself as if apparently he was really making a joke and pulling my leg or talking the way he always did but with so mock a seriousness I believed and trusted and looked at him like the lamb—hate is older than love. I had no objection to acting like a lamb because my mother'd told me so many stories about my little brother died at nine who was so lamby, Gerard, would rescue mice from traps and bring back to health in little cardboard box hospitals that were also cathedrals of holy reverence to which his little face with the soft fall of melancholy hair, over melancholy eyes, turned, impossibly hoping—he made everybody cry when he died, terribly from within. O Russia! Saints in America too!

"Then go home," says Maggie, "I dont care if I dont see you till Sunday."

"Sunday I'll be early—"

"Ah—" waving her hand bitterly, and then suddenly becoming unaccountably tender and sad. "Ah Jack—sometimes I get so tired . . ."

"Of?—"

"Ah never mind." Looking away, with a little pain expression on the corner of her loose, dull smile of heavy womanness . . . too much to carry . . . the freight of her tired, head-nodding understandings of everything that was going on—a woman looks at a river with an expression not-to-be-named. Her rippling mysterious moods, philosophic, rich, faintly bestial like the torture of skulls and breasts of cats, like the drowning of idiots which is what we've come to expect of our spring now, hand loose doubting on hip balanced with head tossing just a little darklashed lowered disbelief and nay, loose ugly grin of self-satisfied womanly idiocy-flesh, curl of travesty-cruelty, I'd want to rip her mouth out and murder her, sudden interior welling-up of tenderness profound, paining, dark, forming milky frowns on forehead, raising moons by the conjuration-fingers up from the bottom of the well which is the womb, nature, black sod, time, death, birth. "Ah go home—Jack—let me sleep. I'm gonna sleep tonight."

"No Maggie, I don't wanta leave when you feel this way—"

"Yes you do—I dont feel any particular way."

"Yes you do—"

"Particular feeling? Just because I just happen sick and tired—of this—and that—what I expect—what *you* expect—I just wanta quit and go home—"

"You are home. There's your door."

Looking at it with a rich frown and a fnuf, "Sure. Home. Okay. Sleep."

"Arent you home?"

"Dream it some other time, so what if it's my home I dont have to get all overexcited about it—"

"I wasnt—"

"You never nothing. Oh Jack—" (pain in her cry)—"go home—stay—do something—I cant *stand* it hanging around day after day not knowing what to do with myself and whether I should get married or not or just—blah—nothing—Oh fer *kri*-sakes, aint you gonna go yet!" (as I'm grabbing her to kiss her)—"Leave me alone!"

Pushing my hand off.

I turn around and walk off into the night.

Four houses down, my neck burning and strangling, in the still winter star solitude she says, distinctly, "Ha ha," and I hear her going in the house, the click of the door, the "ha ha" not laughed but spoken signifies not only she's not through with me but it worked to get rid of me tonight.

I cant face my own conclusions.

I drag along in wonder, hatred, stunned, realizing it's nothing; I go by the cemetery so bemused with these witchery-tortures of whether this, that, Maggie, I dont notice the ghosts, the tombstones, it's just the backdrop now to my anxious hunchings over knuckles.

Three miles home again I walk, in midwinter midnight, this time not fast, or joyous, but dispirited with nowhere to go and nothing in back—all the night does at the end of a street is increase its distance—

Yet in the morning I wake up reconciled with the fact not only she'll make some kind of apology but I ought to laugh and shake it off and shake her off and she'll climb on again.

My mother sees the palings in my thoughts, advises me— "Stop breaking your head on all kindsa junk—concentrate on your track and school, never mind Gus Poulo and your gang they got nothing to do but hang around you got lots of things, see them later, and never mind that Maggie Cassidy—see her this spring or this summer—dont rush things and dont rush around with every-thing and every-body— Take some advice from you old la-dy, aye?" And she'd wink, and pat my head, and reassure me. "I'm not crazy me." Stopped in the middle of the kitchen floor, my

mother, with a kind of ribbon in her coalblack hair, rosy
cheeks on both sides of her big blue eyes, her hands joined
together at her lean rest on the back of the chair just loosely
and for a second, looking at me seriously, primly, grave
understanding of the prime things pressed down in her lips,
and a twinkle in her eyes, "Mama'll always did show you
how to get things done and everything will be all right, I
got you for Saturday night guess what?"

"What? *Quoi?*"

"A nice pair of new shoes, when you go to the track and
change to your sneakers there wont be nobody be able to
say you got old shoes, *tes vieilles son pu bonne*" she'd announce
and sneak in in an entirely different authoritative almost
greedy-sneering believing tone, as a shoe worker she was
talking about the condition of a pair of shoes—"so I got
you a nice new pair at Thom McAns, didnt cost much."

"Aw Ma *tu depense tout ton argent!*" (Aw Ma you spend all
your money).

"*Voyons, ta besoin d'une paire de bottine, ton père itou, fouaire
n'achetez avant l'moi est funi lui itou—weyondonc—*" (Look,
you need a pair of shoes, your father too, have to buy him
some before the month's out too—look here!)—angry such
a thing should not be realized, going off into the parlor to
straighten out a lace armrest on the sofa while we're talking
over my breakfast.

"Ah Ma, I love you" I say to myself, and I dont know
how to say it to her out loud but I know she knows I love
her anyway.

"So *mange*, eat, forget it—a pair of shoes aint no silverware
china bazaar, ah?" And nods, and winks. I sit in the firm
eternity there.

I kneel at my bed at night to pray, instead my head falls
on the blanket and I just goof with my eyes crushed down.
I try to pray in the winter night, moveless.

"Make my skull, my nose, soften, melt; just make me
one piece knowing—"

20

I went to the indoor racetrack that Saturday evening, Pa
was with me, rode the bus down jabbing blah blah blah
"Well so I said to so and so"—

"Hey Pa, *t'en rappelle tu quand qu'on faisa les lions*—Hey
Pa remember when we made the lions, I was four years old,
on Bridge Street, and you'd sit me on your knees imitating
the noises of animals! Remember? and Ti Nin?"

"*Pauvre* Ti Nin," said my father; talk to him, it would
start him, gather in him, "it's a damn shame the way that
poor little girl has found troubles—!"

"—and we'd listen together, you made lions."

"It was fun, I was amusing myself with my little kids,"
he'd say way off brooding darkly, over lost youth, mistaken
rooms, weird troubles and strange gossipy rumors and stiff
unpleasant unhappiness of bleary people in parlors, remembering himself with pride and pity. The bus went downtown.

I explained my track to him, so he'd understand the
night's races better; he understood that 3.7 was my best
time and that night there was a Negro on the Worcester
North team who was supposed to be like a lightning eagle
in the sprints; I was afraid I was going to be beaten in my
city that night by a Negro, just like the young boxers around

the corner at the Crescent and the Rex Ballroom when they put the chairs and the ring in the floor of the cold dancers. My father said— "Go as fast as you can, beat the bastard: they're supposed to run like damn streaks! antelopes of Africa!"

"Hey Pa—and Pauline Cole's gonna be there."

"Oh— That's your other girl? Little Pauline, yeh, I like that little one me— Too bad you dont get along with her, she must be just as good as your little Maggie Papoopy there the other side of the river—"

"They're different!"

"Aw, well you're already startin to have trouble with women!"

"Well, what do you want me to do."

Hand up. "Don't ask *me*! Ask your mother—ask the old curé—ask the askers—*I* dont know—I dont pretend to know— I'm just trying to get along in the world— You'll all have to work with me. You'll see that it's gonna be pretty damn bad, *Comprends?*" loud, in French, like an uncle calling the idiot from the corner making clear to me meanings that can never be recorded in the English language.

Together, heads bent forward with the bus, we rode downtown. He wore a felt hat, I had an earmuff hunting cap; it was a cold night.

The crowd was swarming around the dark street outside the brilliantly lit Annex, it was like some great church service suddenly let out and they were all coming to the track meet, an old church a block away, huge trees, redbrick factory annexes, the back of a bank, the glow of midtown Kearney Square red and vague over the backs of tar roofs and neon signs beyond. The football coach from some little suburban town would be there, talking in the door with the owner of a sporting goods store, or old soda-fountain habitué with long memories of track records from 1915 (like in German Europe); my father and I, bashful, would push through the crowds; my father'd be looking everywhere to see somebody he knew, grinning, and wouldnt see anybody. The mysterious inside, with people standing around the great door to the Annex and the track, beyond them were the boards of the banked turns, like circus props huge and dusty. Ticket takers. Little nameless kids jumping around. "I'll go sit in the stands while I can still get a seat," Pop said. "I'll wave at you when you come out."

"I'll *see you*—" But Pop thinks I said "be seeing you" and is already waddling off through the crowds inside, he walks around the banks, onto the floor, to his plank seat; others are standing in the middle of the track in topcoats jawing. Young kids have already started running around in shorts, when they get older than fourteen or fifteen they'll be getting big hood suits with long running ski pants with the school's colors on them; the older boys are inside leisurely changing. The great mysterious Negro flyer is hidden in the opponents' showers somewhere—like a great lion beast I can feel his stalking presence—like a thonged whip the surly tawny tail is flashing at the level floor, the growl, the teeth, no greeting in the V's and W's of his Vow—the rumbling roar of other lions even further down below— My imagination had been fed on circuses and unclean magazines; I looked everywhere like a goof as I hurried to my track shoes.

Others were there—Johnny Lisle—Dibbick who ran so funny, the track team captain—smells of liniment, towels—

"Hey there Jack waddayasay boy?" Johnny Lisle out of the corner of his mouth. "Think we'll win the 300 tonight?"

"Hope I dont have to run it." It was like the railroad local, it was hard work.

"Melis'll run it tonight—and Mickey Maguire—and Kazarakis."

"Krise, they cant be beat."

"Joe was asking me to run it second man but I dont know that route—you know, I'm a 1000-yard runner, I dont wanta wear myself out and get my *#:! shins all cracked out—"

"I knew I'd have to run it," I said out loud, really complaining, but Johnny didnt hear me as just then a panic seized us all and we knew there was no more time to talk, in twenty seconds we were all bundling in our running hoods and parka pants and stepping out mincingly on little tiny toe-dancer sneakers with hard rubber bottoms to catch the wood of the indoor planks—nail shoes were for moderner high schools with all-cork tracks. In these tight sneakers you could really streak, they were light.

I saw Pauline at the door. She never looked more glamorous, great moist eyes of grueling blue were mooning right at me like swimming seas, at her age it had all the men turning quick furtive felt hats to see her twice. All I had to do was stand there like a post and let her go. She leaned on the wall wriggling before me, with hands back clasped, I just smiled, she made love speeches.

"Hey I bet you'll be watching for me behind the forty-yard line, huh? I'll wave. You wave back at me."

"Okay."

"Dont say that I didnt come here to see you because I dont love ya, see?"—in closer.

"What?"

"I didnt think you'd catch it the first time—I'll get even with you if you grrr with me." She was clenching her teeth and fists at me. All the time she never took her eyes off me; she was in love with something, probably me, probably love. I grieved inside that I had to give up her for Maggie. But I couldnt have Mary and Magdalene both so I had to decide my mind. And I didnt want to be a boor and do the wrong thing hurting Pauline—if boor is strong enough, gross enough. So I looked solemnly at her and said nothing and started out to my race. Her sympathies were with me. "What a funny rat!" she also must have thought—"Never comes and admits nothing." Like Faust.

21

The Worcester men were out, jogging the banks in blue run suits that looked ominous and alien among our red and gray homey suits—and suddenly there he was, the Negro Flyer, long and thin floating on ghost feet in the far corner of the Annex, picking up, laying down his delicate feet with experimental restrain as though when he'd be ready he'd fly like an arrow and all you'd see is the flashing white socks, the reptilian head stuck out forward to the run. Hurdles was his specialty. I was a sunk ghost of a trackman. But, for all his great streaking in wild track meets of indoor New England brightlight night he wasnt going to reckon Jack the white boy, sixteen, hands clasped behind him in a newspaper photo with white kid trunks and white undershirt when early at fifteen I was too young to get a regular track suit, ears sticking out, raw, hair piled inky mass on square

Keltic head, neck line ramrod holding head up, broad pillared neck with base in collarbone muscles and on each side slope-muscled shoulders down to big arms, legs piano thick just above the white socks—Eyes hard and steely in a sentimental Mona Lisaing face—jawbone iron new. Like Mickey Mantle at nineteen. Another kind of speed and need.

The first event was the 30-yard dash. I saw with satisfaction the Negro star wasnt in my heat, which I won from a bunch of kids, breezy. In his heat I saw him win by yards, fast and low and light on his feet, when he reached he clawed for the finish line and not just dull air. The big moment of the final heat came. We didnt even look at each other at the starting line, he too bashful for me, I too beweldered for him, it was like warriors of two nations. In his eyes there was a sure glow of venom tiger eyes in an honest rockboned face, so your exotic is just a farmer, he goes to church as well as you, has fathers, brothers as well as you honestics The Canuck Fellaheen Indian and the Fallaheen Negro face to face in a battle of spears before they hit the long grass, contesting territories that howl around. Pauline was watching very closely, I could see her leaning elbows on knee in the stands with an intent smile digging the whole drama of the track meet and everybody there. In the middle of the track were the officials, with watches, switch lists, we were making our moves by the clock right on schedule with the Lowell *Sun* reporter's written list of events:

30-YARD DASH—*1st Heat (Time: 3.8)—Duluoz (Lowell),*
              Smith (WC)
              2nd Heat (Time: 3.7)—Lewis (WC),
              Kazarakis (Lowell)
              Final Heat   —

This was coming up, he had done 3.7 in his heat, I 3.8 in mine, which meant the difference of a yard, there was no doubt of his tremendous speed. His hands and arms hung loosely and muscular with great black veins. He was going to play beating drums to my wild alto.

We got down on the line, shivering in a sudden cold gust of air from the street; we tested our spit in the planks, kicked at it with dug-in sneakers, stuck the sneaker in and got down like to crawl but on thumb and forefingers level. Bent testing knees, teetered and balanced to feel. Spectators saw the madness of racers—human runners like Greeks of Sparta—the Socratic silences falling over the crowd as the starter raises his gun in the air. To my utter amazement I saw out of the corner of my eye the colored boy laid out almost flat on the floor in a low slung fantastic starting position, something impossibly modern and submarining and subterranean like bop, like the new gesture of a generation. It was in imitation of the great Ben Johnson who ran 60 yards in 6 seconds flat, this kid from the slums of Worcester was mad to imitate him who'd inconceivably broken the world's record by 2/10ths of a second, fabulous ghost streak Negro of Columbia in the late Thirties. Later on in life I'd see American Negro boy imitating Charley Parker and calling themselves Bird on street corners and it would be the same thing, and son to, this gesture of the early bop generation as I immeasurably understood it seeing it the first time. We teetered on thoughtful fingers just on the verge of exploding into fact, bang, the crash from the thought of running to the running itself, the kick-off to the dash. My friend—whose name was some forgotten-by-me Negro name of inconceivable anonymity and humility—

John Henry Lewis was his name—he shot off ahead of the gun and we all flew off in a false start and held up when the gun cracked us to return, he ahead—We reorganized ourselves for the mental anguish of another start. I got down, saw him on my left low and lightly-hung to fly off the floor—and just as I predicted in my own mind the absolute certainty that the starter would shoot he shot but I was already gone. I was flying, luckily legally just barely beat the gun—no one knew but myself and the starter and the starter was Joe Garrity who knew a jump-the-gun when it was illegal and was inflexible (wouldnt cheat) in his knowledge, pity, and sense of duty. I flew ahead of my Negro, my Jim, eyes half closed so as not to see the horror of his black skin at my breast, and hit the tape well ahead but just barely beginning to sense his catch-up as he too late gathered a stunned momentum and knew that he was beaten anyway and by the mind. The others were not altogether out—John Kazarakis who was just coming into his own in realization of what a great athlete he really was hung on John Lewis' shirt behind by some half-inch behind me by a foot and also closing in. But my muscular headlong rush beat the thin speed demons just the same and by sheer will. It was like the way I'd once seen Billy Carr run so fast he stumbled in his run and kept somehow in the air and regained his feet and literally threw himself across the air against the finish-line tape all muscles and white power, 3.5, beating great college sprinters in his high school years . . . Billy Carr that went to Notre Dame, whose glamour in Lowell was some rich and hidden thing in the dense tree mansions of Andover Street in the winter night of golden home lights, lovely girls of summer and finishing schools strolling under laceries of branch in streetlamp sorrows by bushes, drive-ways, iron fences, bandana under pouting lip . . .

My win over John Lewis was received with applause and by myself with awe—as I bounced off the mattress against the wall I looked furtively at John and caught his whites of eye conceding me the race. He even shook his head and said something to me himself like "Man you" or "Damn" and we laughed together as we walked back.

They were putting up the hurdles for the 35, bustles, talk, the reporters typed their results:

30-YARD DASH—Final Heat *(Time: 3.7)*—*Duluoz (Lowell),*
Lewis (WC), Kazarakis (Lowell)

Pauline waved; Pa gave me the okay sign. I'd overcome the ghost. "Ah," I thought, "Ma's gonna be glad—she'll see that I run and work hard and I'm getting to my hand. She'll say to herself, 'Bon, Ti Jean's doing his business, his homework too.'— I'll be able to sit home in the chair not sayin a word all day Sunday— It's at home we win." And I saw my father with joy. "Look at his big happy smile— he's talkin to the men near him— The enemies of my father!—they're far, not near tonight—their mystery doesnt tear my teeth out tonight—the fact that we dont know their face, their place, the savage extent of their indifference to us— We'll bury em a deep one before midnight." My thoughts ran like fallen stars. I saw in my eye in the middle of all the world the dark corners on the floor in my house where my cats, my migs hid, where I'd put my crazy face in rainy afternoons of no-school when I really dreamed im-mortality, the health of my blood and family, the frightening

mystery too. I believed in the planks of the little corner;
I knew that the earth, the streets, the floors and shadows
of life were holy—like a Host—gray, dirty Host of interesting reality (like the bridge at Orleans) of great smoke of
men and things, where I'd find myself an honor so great
that my father with his old coats, humble hat, would look
at me in another heavened life like you look at a man and
we'd speak rare things—"Ti Nin'll read it in the paper, my
sister—she'll show it to her friends— Lousy'll read it tomorrow morning when he gets up to go to church—Scotty—
G.J.—Vinny—"

"And Maggie—"

"I beat the speedy *Neigre* from Worcester—and him, he'll
go back to Worcester—maybe if not to tell to *know* that
in Lowell the guys from the alleys and rock streets run like
demons, let the name of Lowell make a noise in their hearts
after this—that in the world where the name is Lowell the
boys brothers and mad hurl themselves howling in this
mortal ocean . . . brothers, boys, wolves of the North."
(These thoughts were all in French, almost untranslatable.)

I could see all the rooftops of Lowell and Worcester in
my victory, my ideas, sensations. They'd put a poet in my
craw. I was ecstatically insane in my innocence. I knew joys
not by name but that they crossed my clotting breast of hot
blood and disappeared unnamed, unknown, uncommuni-
cated with the thoughts of others but arranged in the same
manner and therefore like the thoughts of the Negro, intent,
normal. It was later they dropped us radar machines in the
sky to derange the senses. Let's hear no more about the
excesses of Rimbaud! I cried remembering the beautiful faces
of life that night.

The 35-yard hurdles I also won flying at the start ahead
of Lewis by that whiteflashing split second—I skimmed over
the hurdles in a mad anxiety, level with the race I dug floors
away, aimed down the line. I was more surprised than
anybody and John Henry Lewis. And for the first time I hit
4.6. I even began to wonder if I'd suddenly become a really
great runner.

22

The track floor was being laid out with broad-jump mats,
high-jump poles, the big shotputters are standing around
agreeing and determining the layout of the jump area so
they can start warming up right away—Ernie Sanderman
who later became a round-the-world magician seaman on
luxurious passenger ships of the blue sea was our best broad-
jumper—stood, on his takeoff board, and swung his arms
back together and wailed out heaving his tortured neck into
the annezvoid-athema of the wild Annex, reaching for his
landing place of both feet he'd jump ten feet, clear across
a narrow livingroom, with big feet flapping to the mark.
I also participated in this event, jumped 9 feet and 5, 6 or
7 inches, made points for the team, but always losing to
Ernie and usually the visiting champ too and finishing
third—

The last event I led off, Kazarakis anchor, the 300-yard
hated relay, with bull-necked Fullback Melis and Irish curly
locks Mickey Maguire from Belvedere, zooming around the
track like streamliners and the Worcester men in their blue

regalia flying a half-foot behind in closepacked races of serious interest, when I was off and underway nothing gave
me a bigger boot than the 300-yard run, it was frantic, you
had to kill yourself, the guys were screaming on all sides,
in the Annex, "Run!" and we'd be hollowy echoing with
hard feet on wood bank board turns making a roar coming
off just on the inside on the smooth basketball floor into
the inside line without now any further booming noise, just
cat feet sprinting, all the mothers of Lowell should have
come to see their sons show their fathers how they can run—
into the woods, into the thieveries and wood piles, into the
hysterical idiot streakfoot madness of mankind—

I took off frightened, the guy with me was a white boy
from Worcester, I let him shoulder me out of the first turn
as we raced with the relay sticks—this was a courtesy on
my part. We boomed around the boards—came off, both
of us, sleekly, skinly, padding up our court, interested
audiences watching interested racers, the whole corps of
newspapermen now alert with heads up from their type-
writers or from the sidelines, a few dull, immediate cries
of opening-lap audiences. "Bang!" the gun had said, the
gunpowder was just spreading in the air—we was off.

My Pop was standing at his bench plank, just bent to
watch, tense, his whole huge body toned to hold up watchful
on the quivering hard legs with which he used to play
basketball in YMCAs of pre-World War I—

"Okay Jean"—under his breath—"Go on!" He was afraid
because I'd given the kid the first bank I'd given up my
show. No. I leisurely followed him around the far turn, and
as we came into the homestretch of the first of two laps I
just passed him with a sneaky quiet sprint he hardly heard

and flew ahead of him bent for that first turn again, for the
tilt of the boards, and flashed by the line of watchers, the
kid was heard to curse, he pictures himself taking off after
me—I was already boastfully in the back stretch and halfway
along it and had done my booming and my soft off-step and
all things of that nature and was in a straight line for the last
turn, no sound, streaking across the kitchen, bent for the last
boards—ghosting in—turning with the world on the revolving banks like a funhouse barrel and now very tired and
hurting all over and my heart dying from so much pain in
lungs, legs—The kid from Worcester overtook nothing, but
lost spaces of breeze between us, hopelessly mawkfaced lost
and discouraged, almost embarrassed to shame. I run up and
assume the handout pose with the relay stick and give it to
Melis with a 10-yard lead and he's off running his two laps
while the next Worcester kid still waits, mincing nervously
on a hot potato—Maguire and Kazarakis complete the race
like invisible bullets and it's a farce, no contest, and relays are
always sad.

—Won races, leaving other boys embarrassed to shame—
Shame . . . that key to immortality in the Lord's
grave . . . that key to courage . . . that key heart. "Lord,
Lord, *Mon Doux, Mon Doux*" (Canadian boy's pronunciation
of *Mon Dieu*, My God) I'm saying to myself. "What's gonna
happen!"—won races, was applauded, laurel-wreathed,
smiled, patted, understood, taken in—took showers,
shouted—combed—was young, youthful, was the key—
"Hey McKeever!" echoing now loud bang in the locker room
glooms. "Hee hee hee didja take a big ass plunge off that 600
fight! Hee hyah ha—whatta batt-ed . . . Jee-heever, ole
Jeeheever sure missed tonight!"

"Kelly? I told Kelly, stop throwing it will ya?"

"Oodja see Smack make that line?"

"Hey, know what happened tonight—"

"Where?"

"Keith's—"

"What?"

"Basketball game—they took on Lowell—"

"What score?"

"63–64."

"Jeez!"

"You shoulda seen Tsotakos—you know, Steve's brother—

"You mean Samaras?"

"No!—not Odysseus, the guy with the red-shirt brother!"

"Spaneas?"

"No!"

"Oh yeah!"

"He's the greatest—they never had a basketball player like him— Nobody talks about him"—(some little kid with thin hands falling under the sleeves of his coat weighing 98 pounds and a class officer and sometime team manager and only fourteen years old bringing back reports from other parts of Lowell in the eventful exciting Saturday night). My father's standing there laughing and getting his kicks from all these funny children and looking around fondly to find me. I'm just putting on my shirt, comb in my hand, making a Hitler mustache at Jimmy Jeeheever with it.

"A great night!" yells an enthusiast from that world-packed Lowell door. "Jimmy Foxx never hit more homers than you guys tonight!"

"Joe Garrity," announces somebody, and here comes our track coach in a shabby sad overcoat sad glinting Harry Truman eyes behind glasses and hands hopelessly folded into his coatpockets and says "Well boys, you did pretty well,

you did pretty well. . . . We scored 55 points. . . ." He
wants to tell us a thousand things but he's waiting for the
reporters and enthusiasts to leave, Joe is very secretive about
his track team and his quiet matter-of-fact grave relations
with each of his boys and all of them in group. "I'm glad
about that win, Johnny. I think you're going to make your
name in Boston Garden before spring." Half grin, half joke,
kids laughing—

"Gee coach, thanks"—Johnny Lisle, who was liked by
Joe particularly because he was an Irish boy and close to his
heart. Melis—Kazarakis—Duluoz—Sanderman—Hetka—
Norbert—Marviles—Malesnik—Morin—Maraski—and
seven Irishmen Joyce McDuff Dibbick Lisle Goulding Maguire, he had international national problems to deal with.
My father, far from rushing up to the coach to be seen with
him, hides in a corner wearing an appreciative smile as he
secretly digs Joe the Coach in his real soul and mentally
pictures him in City Hall and realizes what Joe is like—
and likes him—

"Yah—I can see him at his old desk—like my Uncle Bob
who was that railyard clerk in *Nashué* (Nashua)—trying to
get along with things as best he can— No different than
me— Didnt I know some brother of his a long time ago
on the old *Citizen?* or was it Dowd's out on Memorial Road—
Wal— And whattaya know, Jacky went and beat that
Neigre—ha ha ha—when I saw him there I was sure he was
too fast for him, but he did it! he did it! Ha ha ha, little
tyke, I remember him when he was three feet high and used
to crawl on the floor pushing up boxes to me and bringing
me toys—two feet high—*Ti Pousse!* Ha ha— Say, that *Neigre*
was built, he was sleek—I was damn glad to see my boy

beat *him*—that proves he's an athlete—those *Neigres* are the fastest runners in the world—in the jungles of Africa even right now they're running like mad after wild pigs, with spears—You see it in the Olympics, the great Negro athletes there that Jesse not Jesse James Jesse Jones that Jesse Owens flying—the international flavor of the world—"

Pauline is waiting for me at the door, Pa joins her as soon as he finds her.

"Well by God—Pauline—I didnt know *where* you were— I'da sat with you!"

"Why didnt that damn Jack tell me you were here— Hey!" They loved each other, she always had a joke for him, he for her— Their eyes shined as I rushed out of the showers to join them. It was social, provincial, glad, sad; it was ecstasy in the heart. We felt vibrations of love laughing and yelling in the laughing yelling crowds pouring out and milling around; Saturday night is dense and tragic in all America from Rocky Mount on up, San Luis on over, Killdeer on down, Lowell on in.

"Jack! There you are! Dad," whispering in his ear, "tell that lout we's got a date of our own and we dont want him around tonight."

"Okay keed," my father'd say, puffing on the cigar in a strenuous acting pose, "we'll see if we cant fix him up with Cleopatra next week and make up to him for it." In his jests serious.

"All right, Mark Antony. Or wasnt your name Mark Antonio and you came rovin over here to steal this British baron from my castle?"

"Nah!—we'll shoot him tonight in the stagecoach— Dont

worry about nothing keed. Let's go to Paige's and have an
ice cream soda."

And off we fly, into the bright dry night, stars above the
redbrick snows are keen and clear, knives drop from them—
the big sinewy trees with their claws deep under the pavements are stuck so high in the sky they are like lost silver
in the Up, people walk among streetlamps passing massive
trunk bases of something living and never pay it a thought—
We join the flow of the sidewalks leading downtown—to
the Lobster Cot—Merrimack Street—the Strand—the whole
dense almost riotous inwards of the city aglow for the Saturday night in that time only fifteen years ago when not
everybody had cars and people walked to shop and from
buses to shows, not everything was locked-in strange behind
tin walls with anxious eyes looking out to deserted sidewalks
of modern America now— Pauline, Pa and I could not have
laughed and experienced excitement and jumped so joyously
as we did that night if we'd been in some automobile grimly
buried three in a front seat haggling over traffics in the
window of the television set of Time—instead we loped on
foot over snowbanks, to dry shoveled sidewalks of downtown, to busy revolving doors of wild midnight sodas.

"Come on Jack, you're falling behind. Let's have some
fun tonight!" Pauline was yelling in the street, punching
me, playing with me.

"Okay."

Whispering in my ear: "Hey, did I enjoy your legs tonight! I didnt know you had legs like that! Gee, can I come
and visit you when you have a bachelor apartment? Hey!"

"Say," my father an idea, "how 'bout a nice snack in Chin
Lee's?—some chop suey or something?"

"No let's just have ice cream!"

"Where? In the B.C. or Paige's?"

"Oh anywhere— Gee, I dont wanta get fat Mister Duluoz."

"Aw wont hurt ya—I been fat for thirty years and I'm still here— Wont bother ya."

"Look at Mrs. Madison and her son— You know them Jack, they live next door to me. That little kid always peeking at us?"

"And the dog in the yard with the gray fence?"

"Say"—my Pop—"you two little kids sound to me like you'd make a fine little couple— Why is it ya dont step out together"—laughing in his sleeve—secretly serious.

Pauline "Oh we *used* to go steady Mr. Duluoz." Her eyes misting suddenly.

"Well why dont you now? Just because *Ti Pousse* is supposed to have some sweetie in another part of the county?— pay no attention to him, listen to his old man, psst," whispering in her ear, out of which they explode laughing, and the joke's on me but I tingle all over with joy to be known and loved by them and agree with my father.

Yet suddenly I remember Maggie. She's at the Rex, a stone's throw for me over the neons of Kearney Square and all the dark heads of night and there she is, dancing, with Bloodworth, in the inexpressibly sad musical rose of sunset and moonlight serenades, all I have to do is walk over there, sweep aside the curtain, see all the dancers, look for her form, all I have to do is look—

But I cant leave Pa and Pauline except under some pretext, pretense. We go to the soda fountain, people from the meet are there, also people from the show at Keith's Strand or

Merrimack Square, people from events of social importance
to be mentioned in the next day, you can see their expensive
cars out on the Square, and sometimes right on it (pre-
1942)— My Pa is shabby, crack-toothed, dark and humble
in his big coat, he looks around and sees a few people he
remembers, sneers, or laughs, according to his feelings—
Pauline and I delicately eat our sundaes—because of the
tremendous suppressed excitement to fall down on them
devouring with big spoons— Just a little hometown scene
on a Saturday night—in Kinston on Queen Street they're
driving up and down sadly the Southerners, or walking,
looking in at bleak hardware hay and grain stores, out at
the colored section there's a mob chattering in front of
chickenshacks and taxi stands— In Watsonville California
it's the gloomy mad field and section hands of Mexico strolling, arms sometimes around each other, father and son or
friend and friend, in the sad California night of white raw
fog, the Filipino poolhalls, the town green at the bank—
In Dickinson North Dakota on Saturday night in the winter
it's the howling blizzard, the stalled buses out of town, the
wild warm food and pool tables in great restaurant-lunch-
rooms of the night with pictures of old lost ranchers and
outlaws decorating all the walls— The Arctic loneliness
snowdust swirling on a rill of sage—outside town, the lost
lean fence, the snow moon's fury—Lowell, the soda fountain,
the girl, the father, the boy—the local yokels all around
the local yokels—

"Okay keed," says my father, "and say, do you want to
go home alone with Pauline now or are you coming home
or what?"

"I'll go with her—" I have my big Maggie schemes—I
wink at my father, false. He finds it amusing.

"See you tomorrow keed. Hey, say there goes Gene Plouffe anyway—I'll go along with him in the bus home."

Then, later, I also get rid of Pauline on some other pretense, concerning time, I hardly have room in my raining heart to see and hear what I have to—I'm lost, bumping in the Square crowds. We mill at the bus, I see her "home" to her home bus in front of Brockelman's— Then, in a dream, I rush to the Rex.

It's midnight. The last dance is playing. It's the lights-out dance. Nobody at the ticket office. I rush in, look. It's dark. I see Bessy Jones, I hear mournful saxophones, the feet are shuffling. Last, late sitters in brooding overcoats up in the balcony.

"Hey Bess!"

"What?"

"Where's Maggie?"

"She left at eleven— Bloodworth's still here— She got peeved and went home—alone—"

"She's not here?" I cry hearing the anguish of my own voice.

"No—she left!"

"Oh"—and I cant dance with her, I cant surmount the mountain dream of this night, I'll have to go to bed with the leftover pain of another day. "Maggie, Maggie," I think— It only faintly dawns on me that she got mad at Bloodworth—

And when Bessy Jones yells "Jack, it's because she loves you," I know that. It's something else is wrong, and sad and sick— "Where's my Maggie?" I cry with myself. "I'll walk out there now. But she'll never let me in. Three miles. She wont care. Cold. What'll I do? Night."

The music is so beautiful and sad I droop to hear it

standing thinking lost in my Saturday night tragedy—
Around me all the faint blue angels of romance are flying
with the polkadot spotlight, the music is heartbroken and
yearns for young close hearts, lips of girls in their teens,
lost impossible chorus girls of eternity dancing slowly in
our minds to the mad ruined tambourine of love and hope—
I see I want to hug my Greatshadow Maggie to myself for
all time. Love's all lost. I walk out, to the music, to discouraged sidewalks, disaffected doors, unfriendly winds,
growling buses, harsh eyes, indifferent lights, phantom
griefs of Life in the Lowell streets. I go home again—I have
no way of crying, or of asking.

Meanwhile Maggie's across town crying in her bed, everything is totally unhappy in the grave of things.

I go to bed with horror on my wings. In my pillow is
sad comforts. Like my mother says, *"On essaye a s'y prendre,
pi sa travaille pas"* (We try to manage, and it turns out shit).

23

Morning is when the slackened sleep faces of the children
of God must be righted, rubbed and waked up. . . .

All that day Sunday I mourn in my room, in the parlor
with the papers, Lousy comes to see me and sympathizes
with my face making long drawn glooms on his own ("In
your old town there is nothing much to talk about except
the old saying, 'Dead'," he said actually) but only in between
excited reports of everything that's meanwhile been happening—"Zagg—guess what?—Mouse and Scotty got real
mad the other night and had a big wrestling match at

Vinny's, they almost wrecked the stove, Scotty almost killed him— We played basketball with the North Common Panthers Saturday afternoon when you was resting?—I let em have it, you babe— Seven basket two fouls—sixteen points—I just showed them one of my one-hand side shots, zeet? See M.C. last night at the track meet? I was with my mother'n father at my uncle's— I had a nice girl to talk to, you babe— I said I was gonna bite her ear off— She said *eek!*— Hee hee— Barney McGillicuddy O'Toole was hot Satty, eleven points himself, one a long shot from midcourt, but that team wont be the same, Zagg, till you play again—"

"I will now— I'm through with all this love shit"—

"Kid Belgium Yanny scored two points by god!"

"*Who?*"

"G.J. That's the new name I gave him. Call me 'Sam.' That's my new name. Kindhearted Belgium they also call me. Was M.C. at the meet?"

"Pauline Yeah."

"I see her study periods. Jean," using my French name, "she could even knock out Joe Louis just by lookin at him."

"I know,"—sadly.

"Damn! We shoulda never gone to that damn Rex New Year's Eve! Everything changed since then! Even me!"

"Take it easy, Kid Sal Slavos Len!"

"Well ga-dammit I'm mad!" jumping off the bed with the sudden furious funny small-eyed rage of a mad cat. "Eh? Mad! Hey Zagg?"

"Kill em, Sal, dont let em get you down."

"I'll bury em a mile deep!" Lousy swung at the air. "King of the Tits!"

The rest of the gang filed into my room, my mother'd

let them in from the front; it was gray Sunday, symphonies on the radio, papers on the floor, Pop snoring in his chair, roast beef in the oven.

"Good old Belgium!" yelled Vinny embracing Lousy. "Scot, show Zagg your contract. He made out a contract to make us promise to help him buy that car next summer."

"Beware if not signed—Signed, the Unknown, that's what it says, Zagg," put in Gus who also was gloomy this day, green, quiet, musing.

Lousy had his fists up before him. "Fight? Fight?"

"The contract?" chuckled Scotty showing his cunning gold tooth. "We will discuss the deal under a few liquidoriums."

With a cat's furious rage raining sweats Lousy was still dancing shadowboxing.

G.J. looked up. "Did you bring that paper Vinny?"

"No—the storm stopped me, I threw it away." Snow outside.

"Lookout!"

G.J. jumped up suddenly with his knife, and placed it in Vinny's back. "The bastid! He'll get shithouse and kill us all!" screamed Vinny.

"Just like Billy Artaud—you know what he said the other night, 'Sorry Mouse I cant help you clean up the Silver Moon saloon gang Depernac's gangsters because my left vertebral artebral is injured'— Wattaguy!"

"This spring every one of you guys is gonna lose his head, I'm gonna pitch and bean you with my new high hard one— Opening day, March!"

Scotty:—(musing aloud) "It'll be wind like a bastid out and it'll be pretty hard to judge those balls that first afternoon and maybe the sun'll be shining and the only thing that'll be wrong is that wind—"

"Sure!"

"Zagg"—Gus solemn—"when I bean you the first time you'll be staggering and reeling at the plate and I'm going to bean you again!—a broken heap they'll see you Pitou Plouffe and the gang groveling to your home in sunset— easy prey to my more blinding than ever speedball and loping curve—" In actuality Gus's pitching was the biggest hilarious in the gang, he had so little control one time he threw a pitch over the backstop and we never found the ball again as it probably rolled down the hill to the river—

We tried to continue and expand these conversations; at suppertime they left. Grayness covered Lowell, the jokes were said, the goofs done— Something was like loss on mute snowbanks in the streets; and here in the long dark light of late day you'd see the litle kids coming back from Sunday afternoon movies tripping from double features at the Royal and the Crown— Sunday night came with one wink of streetlamps—I mooned in the club watching bowlers—I walked in the sad finished-up streets of human time.

Monday morning we blearily blearyfaced met and proceeded to school as usual— Heartbrokenly I could hear the song *I'm Afraid the Masquerade is Over* darkening in my ear as we crossed the windy bridge— All the joy was gone from my anticipation of days—

But in the Spanish class, lo!—a note from Maggie.

I tore it open, slow and thoughtful, shaky.

Dear Jack,

I am writing this Saturday night after the dance. I feel very blue and let me explain. Bessy came over to me, Bloodworth introduced

her to Edna. And you know how I like Edna and her smug ways.
She said Pauline was with you at the track meet. Well I flew right
off the handle. Edna and Pauline are friends and they would stop
at nothing to get you away from me. You made me so jealous I dont
know what I said or did all I know is that I wanted to get out of
there but the girls wouldnt come home with me. If you have to talk
with Pauline please dont let any of my friends see you because it
always gets back to me. I cant seem to get over my jealousy it must
have been born in me. And of course there is another side to the
story. In my jealousy I do things that hurt you and that is the last
thing I want to do. I cant seem to understand that you can go out
with any girls you want to without me having to interfere. I realize
now how selfish I have been. Jack you will have to forgive me please.
I think it is because I like you so much. I will try and remember
that it is your privilege to go out and do as you please. I'll be jealous
of course but I have to get over it sometime. Some day you might
find in me the qualities you admire most in a girl and a selfish one
at that. I know you have every reason not to answer but, you always
let me get away with too much and I knew it. I just had to write
and tell you I felt so sorry about the other night.

                              With all my love
                              MAGGIE

Please forgive me

                                        Write soon—tear this up.

   That night I was there at eight o'clock, immediately after
supper and on the fastest bus, the gloomy air had turned
warm, something had broken and mushroomed in the wet
winter earth of Lowell, ice was cracking on the Concord,
winds blew with a greeny freight of hope over excited trees—
it seemed the earth was being reborn— Maggie ran into my
arms at the door, we hid in it in the dark silent and tight
held, kissing, waiting, listening—"Poor Jacky, you'll never
have anything but trouble with a damn fool like me."

"No I wont."

"I got sore at Bloodworth the other night. Did you see him? Today? At school? Can you tell him I'm sorry?"

"Sure—sure—"

Hiding her face in my sweater "I've been feeling awful anyway— My uncle died, I saw him in his coffin. Ah—it's so . . . people tell me I'm bored, I shouldnt hang around the house thinking about boys—about *you—you*," kissing me poutingly—"I dont even wanta *leave* the house—if all they've got is coffins, dead—How could I work I dont even wanna live. Oh my—I was so skeered—"

"What?"

"My *uncle*—They buried him Friday morning, they dropped rocks on him and his flowers—I was feeling bad about you anyway—but that's not what was wrong—but I cant tell you—explain you—"

"Nevermind."

She sat staring on my lap for hours, silent, in the dark parlor—I understood everything, held myself in, waited.

24

And that Saturday night when I met her at the Rex, as our usual arrangement, they were playing *The Masquerade Is Over* when she came in with Bessy from the cold—ineffably beautiful as never before, with dew drops in her black hair like little stars in her eyes, and rosiness effulging from sweet laughs tinklin one after another— She was feeling good again, beautiful and unwinnable again forever—like the dark rose.

Her coat smelling of winter and joy, in my arms. Her coquettish looks everywhere—impulsive quick looks at me to laugh, comment, or criticize, and straighten my tie. Suddenly throwing her arms around my neck and pulling up her eyes to my face, her own, seized like a sob to squeeze me, plead love out of me, own and possess me greedily, whispering in my ear— Cold wiggling nervous hands in mine, the sudden grip and fear, the vast sadness all around her like wings—"Poor Maggie!" I thought—looking for something to say—and there is nothing to say—or if you said it—it would fall like a strange wet tree from your mouth—like the pattern of black veins in the earth of her uncle's and all uncles graves—non-sayable—non-ownable—split.

Side by side we stared at the dance, the two of us dumb and darkened. Adult love torn in barely grownup ribs.

25

Maggie by the river—"Poor Jack," sometimes she laughs, and fondles my neck, looks deep into my eyes rich and snug—her voice voluptuously breaking on a laugh, low—her teeth like little pearls in those red gates of her lips, the rich red gates of summer's fat, April's scar— "Poor Jack"— and now the smile has faded from the dimples, only the light of the smile flashes in her eye—"I dont think you know what you're doing."

"I wouldn't be suss-prised—"

"If you knew what you were doing you wouldnt be here."

"Didnt I say so."

"No—you didnt say so-o-o—" rolling her eyes drunkenly at me, making me drunk, passing her cold palm over my cheek in a sudden caress so tender the winds of May would understand and the winds of March wait back for, and the soothe "oo" of her lips making some silent little blow word to me, like "oo" or "You"—

My eye'd fall looking right in hers—I wanted her to see the windows of my secret. She accepted it—she didnt accept it—she wasnt decided—she was young—she was cautious— she was moody—she wanted to reach something in me and hadnt done it yet—and maybe that was enough for her, to know—"Jack's a dope."

"I'd never have anything with him—He'll never be a hardworker like we see, like men, around, Pa, Roy—he's not our kind— He's strange. Hey Bessy, dont ya think Jack is kinda strange?"

Bessy: "N-a-w ? ?—How could *I* know!"

"Well—" Maggie humphin with herself—"I dont know, I must say," turning to camp at teacups, "I rally daont knaow." On the radio, record programs. Pillows all over. If I could have played hooky in *that* parlor. Sunny drapes— morning.

"So ya made up with Jack, huh?"

"Yeah." Rich-throated, like the modiste that's older than the other, like you see great old women in San Francisco bleak wood tenements sitting all day with their parrots and old cronies talking about when they owned all the whore-houses of Hawaii or complaining about their first husbands. "Yeah. I dont think he'd think much of me."

"Why?"

"I dunno. I told you he was kinda funny."

"Ah you're crazy."

"I guess I yam."

If I'd laugh, and throw love teeth in her face, the big grin of accepting rapportive joy, she'd have just a twinge of suspicion of my motives—which would deepen—all night—till the bottomless sorrows of the dark—all my dark walks back from her house—all our misunderstandings— all her schemes, dreams—floop—all gone.

26

My birthday party was coming up but I wasn't supposed to know about it—all planned by my sister, to be had in a little cottage up the Pawtucketville hill near the church, her girlfriend's house. It was all supposed to be hidden from me. Presents were bought—little Emersonette radio so auspicious then but later to be little radiator radio of my father's dull flops in cheap hotels in the years to come of his wandering work— Baseball glove, supposed to be mark and symbol of the coming baseball season and all of us to play ball, bought for my birthday by Bloodworth probably— neckties— Everybody was invited by my sister:—Maggie, Bloodworth, Lousy, Iddyboy, a few of her friends, my parents, girls from the neighborhood the boys would bring with them— I wasnt supposed to know about it but I did.

Bloodworth told me.

One night our friendship deepened immensely and sensationally in front of the Giant Store, across from the Silk Mills, the canal, in front of Boys' Club, we'd been talking since practice where he came sometimes to see me run and now aimlessly walking to continue talk had reached the compromise split-up point of "I go home this way you go home that way"—to supper— It was already dark, cold winter, the streetlamps of the street bright like diamonds in cold howly grit winds, unpleasant— We hung there just talking— And about Maggie, baseball, everything—To keep warm we just suddenly began playing imaginary catch from about five feet from each other showing our also demonstrative technique styles of catch and throw, the leisurely windup, the throw—"Big leaguers always lob the ball easy" said Charley "you go to Fenway Park and you see the guys before game time just pitching it in easy not one guy throwing to snap and it looks like no effort at all but they can throw the ball far with the same easy lob, from years of easy lobbing— This means 'Dont throw your arm out' "—

"Charley, you shoulda been a big leaguer."

"I'm gonna be—I hope—I'd sure love it—Taffy'll make it—Taff will—"

In histories of their own in the Lowell Highlands Bloodworth and Taffy Truman had bent their heads together over their tremendous personalities and hope, ambitions, reading papers over each other's shoulders, rushing to games, broadcasts, known each other's most personal impossible interior hang-up pose core like they'd know their own or the marks of their own wounds— In coldwind nights stalked in jackets talking, like Scotchmen in an Edinburgh of the New World— Both of them worked on the railroad in Billerica, and their fathers too—

"Taff will make it—big leagues—I aint worried, Bill— Here's the way I wind up and throw—"

"Here's how my crazy pal G.J. Rigopoulos?—pitches,

he's the craziest guy in the world" I yelled to him across
the winds and showed him, the Bob Feller exaggerated
windup of almost falling back to the ground to throw, long
leg up.

On Moody Street we're pitching the invisible game the
week of my birthday party, now we were imitating a great
battery, I was squatted down with imaginary catcher's mitt,
we had ghost batters up and whole innings to play. "Two
and O, two on, weary Charley Bloodworth pitching a crucial
ninth—peppery sensational Jack Duluoz behind plate—
here's the pitch—I think you should know they're gonna
throw a party for ya—your sister—"

"Who? *me?*"

"Yeah, boy. Maybe you'd drop dead from excitement or
shock or something, I dont know—I dont like surprises
myself—so when March twelfth comes just take it easy and
you'll see—Your sister and M.C. Number One've been talking on the phone for weeks. You got lots of nice presents
boy—including one I aint gonna tell you about—"

My mother and father were deeply involved in the big
party too, it was arranged for cakes, for a newspaper reporter
to be there, games. I didnt look forward to it because of
the immensity of everything. I half guessed that I would
have to act surprised and as if I didnt know when everybody'd
yell "Happy Birthday!" I bit my lips . . . proud.

27

The big night came.

Everybody was off to the party to await my arrival. I sat alone in the kitchen waiting for Iddyboy to come—"eediboy, come on, my brother Jimmy want to see you about something!" Jimmy Bissonette, the man of the house where the shindig was about to bang—friends of my sister— Outside a huge blizzard has started, by midnight it will have paralyzed Lowell and be making history 20 inches deep, vast, prophetic. How sad and funny that my parents are hiding with fun hats and our own house is empty— I have all the lights out, wait by the window among empty window shades, dark lost coats— I'm all dressed to go in my high school football sweater with the "38" on it for 1938 and a great sewn-in "L" for "Lowell" a little football sewn in redly in the gray thread of the "L"—an undershirt beneath, no collar—I want to have my picture taken by the photographers they'll call from the local papers, I foreknow— Everybody else will wear coats, vests, ties—I'm going to look like an absurd child whose gray dream of vanity even love cannot penetrate.

I look out the window at the tremendous storm gathering.

Through it, eager gleeful big good Iddyboy's plodding gravely to the plan—I see him in specky sweeps across the Gershom arc lamp rounding the corner, bent, his shoes leave little idiotness dots in snow, goodness tramps in the ghost and glee of it—my chest stabs deep sweet transcendent pain to see it, him, the snow, the night—across the furying murks thirty persons are hiding to scream me Happy Birth-

day, Maggie among them— Iddyboy rolling along in the
slanty glooms, his big sleeky grin in sleet, teeth shining
small separate gleams, rosy, glad, shadows in his rugged
ruddy hardbone nose—an old pro guard of beef and iron
slung low to murder when smash-football breaks the ruddy
turfs—his busty knuckle knob of fists inbent in stiff sartorial
partygoing gloves— "Bash I boo!" he says—he reaches out
a snap punch and bashes the picket fence clean off the base—
says "Grargh" and goes *vlup* and pelts his picket off—as oft
he'd under cold midnight streetlamps dared me to try it,
pow!—life in the nailed-in picketpost holds still, my knuckles burn, I try two more times, "Hard! sharp! ye boy!"—
some oldwood frozenness cracks, the picket flies off—we
range along the fence casting tooth after tooth out of it,
crack, Old Man Plouffe who lived across from our favorite
parkfence a strange old idler who'd all he do is open windows
in the middle of the Lowell Night and admonish the boys
"*allez-vous-en mes maudits vandales*!" with his stocking cap
and rheumy rosy eyes alone in his brown house by forlorn
coffin strips velvet and spittoons he'd hear the crack of our
pickets at 2 A.M. — Iddyboy's dark leer at the thought of
it— "Hoo Gee!" yelled Iddyboy the night the French Canadian Mayor won the Lowell election, Arsenault O golden
name, Iddyboy in political excitement leaped up from our
fifteen-year-old pinochle game when my parents were out
in the dense Lowell night and crammed his fist through the
plaster of the kitchen wall, a prodigious wallop enough to
kill Jack Dempsey gloveless like that—the plaster caved in
on the other side in the radio mahogany table room—when
my mother came home horrified she was convinced he was
a maniac and worse— "He put his fist through it? His

boot!" Knuckle marks were sunk in the deep wall. "How did he do that! I tell you they're all crazy the Bissonettes— they've got the damnedest men in that family—the father—" Iddyboy, calmed down now—momentarily stops at the wood fence below, I see him turn anxious haggardness four flights up in the soft spit snow to see—"What? No light? Jacky aint dey? Where's that damn He Thee Boy! I'm gonna break that neck! Argh"— He plunges across the street and under my sight at the tenement doors, powerful, silently sore, I hear him barge in the halls, Iddyboy is swimming up to me in the gloom of a dream so huge I see there is no end to it, to me, to him, to Maggie, to life, to wife, to world—

"Kid you big Marine!"—our greetings at the door.

"Come on boy, my brother Jimmy wants to see something about you—"

"What?"

"Oh"—trying to look unconcerned, with heavy tragic eyes falling—"he's nothing, you babe. Come!"

He explodes laughing "Hee!" He squeezes my knee, we sit facing, hard iron racks enclose my knee as we sleek teeth at each other in the continuation of the Eediboy Marines burlying down the planks of the bridge— I feel like saying "I know about the party, Ye Boy" but I dont want to disappoint his big believing heart— We look at each other, old friends. "Come on you lad. Hat! Coat! Less go!"

We bend to the blizzard, go up Moody— Suddenly the moon wheels pale in a crack of penetrative clouds—"Look, the moon!" I cry—"Iddyboy you still believe that man in the moon with the basket of twigs?"

"Those black shapes not eyes! Not a basket of twigs, a

bundle!—It's wood—*du bois*—Your eye dont believe what
you see? It's you moon, kiddo Ti Janny, all the hopeful
people knows that!"

"*Pourquoi un homme dans la lune? Weyondonc!*" (Why a man
in the moon? Come on!)

"Ey, ey," ominous to stop, leaning hand on knee, "dont
talk like that—it's true *weyondonc*. You're afraid you? You's
crazy? Ah? *Tu crais pas?* You dont believe? On your birthday?
Dont you do believe?" Iddyboy who in church on Sundays
stood straight as a post in front pews of Sainte Jeanne d'Arc
turning bulging red faces when loud noises disturbed the
silent priest in his silent altar—Iddyboy wanted no pretense
in this world.

"It's not true all that!"—firm atheistic adolescent denials
I make.

"Non non non! A man in the moon needs that bundle
of wood!" he says angrily—shudders hugely in his mighty
chest— "Ah gee-boy!"—simple-minded, without alteration
sprung from the blood of the pure paisans of the North, the
noises issuing from his throat the refined gutturals of an
eloquence to tell—"Me I believe in *Le Bon Dieu*, Jacky"—
palm up—"He bless me, make me, save me—" He takes
my arm, friendly—"Hey!" he yells suddenly remembering
the swishy sissy girl of Gershom Avenue who flew along the
kiddie sidewalks of dust red ridden dusk flapping his behind
with one dainty wink at the hole in the sky, Iddyboy says
"I'm So So Su Su that kid there we see flashipott arouns—
I'm a sissy boy too!" and he wiggles off with his powerful
butt like iron cannons in coat storms and minces with his
nail of a finger in the cold night— He comes back, puts
his arm around me again, laughs, conducts me up the street

and to the party believing in me—says, loud so you can hear two blocks up, "Argh, we are *good* friends, ey?"—he shakes me, makes me see love in Heaven, makes me ope my stupidness and innocence eyes—his cheeks rich, red, hotnecked to go and sleek up the world through his happy teeth—"See, you babe?"

28

We climb the steps of the little bungalow, there's just a kitchen light inside, we go in, Jimmy his older brother is smiling at us from the middle of the linoleum— There's a kitchen, livingroom, diningroom, one extra bedroom made by the childless young couple into a rumpus type room— Strange silence—

"Take off your coat and rubbers Jack," they both instruct me. I do so.

Out of the rumpus room comes a great shriek of voices "Happy Birthday!!!" My father bursts out, followed by my mother from another room, Bloodworth and Maggie from another, my sister Nin behind, Jimmy's wife Jeannette, Lousy, Taffy Truman, Ed Eno, others—a swim of faces in my eternity—the house roars. "Wheee!" fiendishly shouting Jimmy is opening a quart of whisky, pushing it at me—I take a burning swig to roars— A great cake emerges, with candles— The opening festivities—I blow them out— Cheers! We're standing yelling eating cake in the kitchen—

"Give the guest of honor a big piece there! Put some

weight on him for next fall!"—laughter, a girl's screech of delight from beyond, I've had no time to say hello to Ma or Pa or Maggie in the crowd excitement, the too-much world— I see Iddyboy trying to be social like in movies the cake in his big paw laughing with Martha Alberge his girl and he lets out a big explosive Phnu! of laughter that kicks in his big battering-ram belly and blasts up his throat and out comes spewing a streamer of snivel all over the cake— nobody sees, he falls, kneels on the floor, holds his belly laughing— His fantastic brother Jimmy is screaming excitedly some dirty joke, my father is doing the same thing near the stove, the house-top shivers maniacally in the great now-howling swept-over blizzard, heat beats at the windows, I grab Maggie by the waist, I yell— Door opens, fresh arrivers—red shouting faces turn to it as new people fall in. Roars of approval, applauses, raisings of bottles— "Oh Ti Jean," my Ma is shouting in my ear, "there was supposed to be millions of your school friends here tonight!—Ti Nin fixed you a grand party—not half of em came—you shoulda seen the list she made with Maggie—"

"Maggie too?"

"Sure! Oh Jacky"—mournfully gripping me, flushed, her best cotton dress, white ribbon in her hair, she adjusts my T-shirt under the huge hot idiotboy sweater, "it's an awful storm, the radio's saying it's the biggest in years—"Then gleefully: "Sssst gimme a big kiss and hug, and hey shh dont tell nobody but here's a five spot I'm slippin you aye?— *tiens*—that's for your seventeenth birthday take in a good show and a big spree on ice cream, invite Maggie to come with you— Ah pet?"

"Boo hoo hee ha ha!" Jimmy Bissonette let out his mad maniac laugh you could hear three blocks away soaring over the blabbers and hubbubings, I stared in amazement, they'd told me this man many a night in wild Lowell afterhours'd challenge anyman to have a bigger one that he had and show how he could shove seven or eight or nine or ten quarters off a table with his piece, all amid roaring laughters of wildparty Canadians of lake cottage clubs in crazy lurid summer with ivy blue moon on the lake or winter when the piano music, smoke, shouting and leaping took place behind bleak shutters and pale reeds creak in stiff ice (the unused divingboard)—to bets, screeches, Tolstoyan hurrahs and huzzahs of revel night—Jimmy insane for girls—on strong squat legs he rushed with wildsweat joy around the wooden bars of Moody, in clubs at spectral orange houseparties with telegraph wires outside the bay window (Ford Street, Cheever Street)—his ears stuck out—he raced anxiously—his feet rapidly scissored fast little steps—you'd see just the proud raised head the bursting gargling eediboy joy then the long-waist body underneath pumped along by whirring feet . . . spats sometimes, lost Saturday nights of French Canadian ecstasy—

And there's my father, in the press he's only roared, coughed, shouted his own partying words from behind knotted groups of the kitchen—he's in this big new brown suit, his face is dark and almost brick red, his collar wilting, necktie raggedly hopelessly rattysnarled and twisted at his tortured sweaty neck—"Ha ha dont give me that stuff Maggie!" arms around her squeezing her, patting her behind "I know you never showed them the way to wear a bathingsuit I sure am sure you should of!" (Huge cough)—the which Maggie weathers unblinking like detonations— At the windows watchers Aw and OO the storm—

"Gonna be a pippin."

"Look at those big thick flakes falling straight down. Sure sign."

"Yeah with a high wind comin up always means a big whopper—"

"Well let's have a little song someone!—Hey Jimmy sing em your horse song your dirty song!"

"A high school party! Take it easy! Moo hoo hoo hwee ha ha!"

Vinny, G.J., Scotty show up, in big coats, scarfs, with girls, late—the storm— Friends of the family pour in whooping, snow flakes, bottles—the party's wild. Charley Bloodworth's three buddies Red Moran, Hal Quinn and Taffy Truman from the Highlands grimly sit in a corner, the French Canadians yell in French, the boys hear it with rat-tat-tat disbelief, composts and rim-posts, jabberous, impossible—my father yelling "Okay let's talk English so we can chat with Bloody and the boys here—buncha ballplayers you know—say Red, wasnt your father the old Jim Hogan that had that meat market up on whattayacallit Square off Westford Street, you know the one I mean—"

"No," shouting back, "no Mister Duluoz it's an old relative of ours had that store—Luke Moran not Hogan—"

"I remember him—had that little store a few years earlier near West Street—old Maria was his wife—he had jews harps hanging on his wall— Years we traded there. Centreville."

"I dont know who that is—"Red's skeptical. "No—"

They cant come to an understanding who Red's father

is—Taffy Truman the great young pitcher sits, hands closely joined, waits.

Beside him Harold Quinn the hero of Bloodworth's breed and hill, I'd seen him calf-bulgant on second base in dusty Twi League eves on South Common, the crack of the bat, ball skitters in rough patch grass of second base, Harold Quinn's stepped over and scooped it up with an authoritative glove, has swept it off to first quickly beginning a double play, hustles back to his keystone sack, taps it with a cleated foot, waits, the runner slides to him in field dust clouds, he clombs up the low throw in his glove for the downward unassuming putout tap on the fellow's shoulder, pulls back his left foot turnaway from kicking spikes, spits silently between teeth as the dust starts spreading, his little spit spurt hangs in midair, falling into the dust, the man is OUT— Beside him Red Moran bends forward in his chair holding a small strawhat toy from the rattles of the party—

Bang, crash, all my Lowell raving wild.

29

Heat generates to the ceiling. Vapor in the windows. The wild windows of other houses and Saturday night parties shining the spilling molten hot gold of real life. I'm sweating, the big athletic sweater is killing me, making me hot, wetfaced, sad at my own party. In the kitchen the older folks are already half in the bag, rounds of nips, drinking songs; in the rumpus the youngsters start a post office game with gleeful couples running into the cold dark blizzard

windowed unheated parlor to neck. Maggie is the star.
Bloodworth, Moran, Quinn, Truman, Lousy even, everybody's rushing her in and out of the parlor for passionate
kisses—my face burns with jealousy. I rush her in when the
spin-bottle points at us—

"You're kissin Bloodworth like mad tonight."

"Aint we sposed to, dope? That's the rules."

"Yeah but he enjoys it—you enjoy it—"

"So?"

"So—I feel—" I grab her, shivering; she fights out.
"Never mind."

"Old jealous. Let's go back—"

"Why right away?"

"Cause—I'm cold in here—Lissen! They're laughin!" And
she rushes back into the heated rooms, I follow emptily
reaching. Alternately cold and hot, the next time we hit
the parlor she flies into my arms and bites my lips and I
feel tears in my ears, wet—"Oh Jack, love me tonight! All
those fellers are after me!—that Jimmy felt me up—"

"Dont let em!"

"Oh you lunkhead—" Hugging herself at the whited
windows. "Look the blizzard has put a sheet of snow on the
pane—God I wonder if my father had to go out and work
in this muck—I oughta call home— Maybe Roy's car'll be
stuck—"In my arms, curled, brooding:—"Did you hear
about one of the Clancy triplets dying gee it was one of
those things a sore throat and she died within a day—I
could tell you a lot about it but it's really heartbreaking so
let's forget about it—"

"You always follow the bad news around South Lowell
always always."

"I'm just so skeered somethin'll happen to my family—
Did you hear about Eddie Coledana too? You know Eddie
he's in the hospital a freight elevator fell from the fourth
floor in the Suffolk Knitting Mills Company where he was
a weaver, something went wrong, the elevator was falling
the freight in it fell on top of him isnt that awful? Oh why
do I think of it now at your party?"

"Maggie—Maggie—"

"How's the kid?"—in my ear—"Love of my life—"

"Am I, honest?—what would I have done if you hadnt
come to my party—"

"Are you mad?"

"No—nah."

"—that's the question before the house. Oh," sighing,
"I guess I'm just a scatterbrain." Voluptuously gloomy in
my hopeless arms. I'm afraid to say any more to bore her.
Wild, everybody talking to me, through human mazes all
night I try to struggle to her—knowing that I'm losing her
now—Lousy has me by the arm trying to cheer me up; he's
beginning to see; I feel his love for me, man to man, boy
to boy, "Aw Jack, easy you babe, easy—you know dont you
that I'm still saying that was the best dinner I ever had up
your house Sunday, ah?—why it even beats the hamburgers
you made last summer— Just for me! You goodhearted Jack!
I came in the house, you woke up, you put a half-pounda
butter in the frying pan, big pats of meat, zzzt, big smokes,
onions, katchup—zeet? The greatest cook in the world!"

Together we watch Maggie rushing off into the parlor
with Bloodworth, Red Moran pulling her the other way—
I feel like sawing those boys through a crack in the Scotch
wood of the Irish Revolutionary doorjamb—

"It's all right, Zagg, she's a young foolish girl having a big time—I didnt kiss her I laughed—I *laughed*! Hee hee! Just a girl, Zagg, just a girl. Next week we down our parafanelyers for a little training, right?—*baseball*! Things are dishing out! Iddyboy our faithful pal will be catcher, Kid Babe Sam me on third base—just like as always, nothing changes you babe!"

"Demand your rights!" yells Scotty joining us, in the middle of the room we stand wound-in-arms touching heads.

"Scot on third—G.J. the magnificent on the mound—a great season of funny games!—All's well!"

Gus joins us—"Zagg I dont wanta say anything but Maggie Cassidy just sat on my hand and wouldnt get off, I tell you I was never so embarrassed in all my life I swear on my mother's name—and she wouldnt budge! And that huge Emil Blooah your father he sure does look at a girl's ass when she walks away but all the time when she's sittin on his lap he's tweaking her chin and saying jokes you know? Zagg what could he do?—he'd kill a girl just by laying on top of her— You shoulda seen how huge his eyes popped! I was scared for Maggie. I warn you Zagg, Frank Merriwell your arch foe has slipped me a couple bucks not to tell you this—"

Lousy: "When this party is over, my friendlies, I'm goin home, you know how the bed feels." In my ear whispering: "Pauline's deeply in love with you, Jack, no shit! She's been raving about you every time I see why even yesterday in my spare as I came in the room she ask me if I wasnt gonna do my homework, I said part of it— Boy I never touched my books for the rest of the period. Asking questions here and there— She even said I laugh like you, I talk like you, the same motions. She said if you ever get fatter she is too. Honest Jack she's even talking about the future. She's going to marry you and everything you possibly can think of. I'm not supposed to say this according to what she says. She asks me a lot of questions. She asks me if you have any other girlfriends. She dont mention Maggie. To make it look good on her side I said 'No' in a slow voice—I wish I had a whole day to myself so I could tell you all what she says. Listen you sneaking rat what did you tell Pauline that first Sunday you went up to her house—last November after the game— Dont say nothing face to face? Well I know different, she says to me 'Oh I know something about you,' she said, 'you should be ashamed—' Give the full details— Ah? confess what you said!" I'd told her about Lousy and I demonstrating that first kiss. "So long you sneaking Belgium Babe! I'm going to dream up some black angels in my nice white pillow now you babe— What a storm for sleep!"

"Zagg," said G.J. philosophically and brotherly arms around me in the roar, "remember our fights in the hall? You'd call me from outside—'Yanny!—innocently I'd come down like a normal human being but you were hiding in the dark, eyes gleaming, breathing heavily, pouncing on me— Yesterday I saw everything different, the time you twisted my arm and it cracked I shot a left hook to your body, you wavered under the impact but came back fast with a right cross to the jaw— I retaliated with a sharp left and jab to the groin and boy did you groan—weaving and dodging I came in fast for the kill—shooting four lefts and seven rights I brought you down to your knees, then faster than an eye wink I went for my iron and conked you over the head. A surprised look came over your face, you tried to clamber to your knees—which was your downfall—lifting all strength I swung my john high over my head and bringing it down hard on your dome I felled you like an ox— Ah what a life!" suddenly gloomy. "Happiness'll disappear, bitter grouchy and dont care will come back ever in this ga'dam world. But what the krise if it makes God happy then there's no harm in it— All our dreams, Zagg, childhood together—things like the fights in the hall— Now you're grown up, your Ma fixed you a big birthday party, your girl's here, your father, your friends— Yes dont kid yourself Jack, there is still some kind people left in this world— You may some day be ashamed but dont ever be ashamed of me, what we've known together, us, in our screwy talks and adventures—look at Lousy, good old Belgium going home to sleep—in a minute he'll be headin up Riverside in the blizzard as a thousand times I seen him from my kitchen window and cursed that the world was black, all's right with the world and Lousy self-satisfied and holdin himself in is going to his well-deserved rest—there you have it, Zagg."

Scotty all combed, suited, smilefaced: "You babe if you cant be good be careful—heh heh heh! Till Saturday at 5 P.M. I'm workin now and especially Friday night till 11 P.M.—Vinny got kilt the other day when he hit a hole with Zaza's bike his leg got scratches and four fingers and I think personally he's puttin some on— See him? He's gonna get a big job in Lawrence now carryin huge bundles of cloth on his shoulders from morning till night— But this summer we'll all be together again and have a jaloppy this time and go swimmin after games—"

"I hope so, Scot." Later, by woodstoves, we'd grimly add it all up, together a thousand miles apart.

Firmly he places his arm around me, smiles.

I close my eyes, I see little Puddinhead Bunky DeBeck in his infant wear big sunflower lace sitting in his cookiebox in Saturday night color-selection cartoons "Fagan youse is a Viper" he complains to big bedeardoed huge hunkey Chaplin Fagan with big bum's lips replying "Why is I a Viper, Bunky!" as he climbs out the window with a mask in the sad red print— Maggie's dancing wildly, I sit gooping—

Across the party my Ma comes running gleefully hunching her shoulders biting her tongue to throw long embraces around me, wants to show everybody how much she loves her boy, yells "Hey there Jacky what you say Mama's gonna come and give you a big kiss!" smack!

The photographers come, everybody's screaming instructions sweatingly two group photos are arranged— In the first one I stand between Ma and Pa, Bloodworth Truman and Moran sit to the left representing fellow high school athletes gravely and with glints in their eyes, Jim with arms around his buddies, Jimmy Bissonette sits to the right with his wife Jeannette, hosts— Jimmy is simpering up his face into the camera about to burst goo gool gee ha ha his crashing laughter, all excited in a tightfitting French roué coat like the European coats of pornographic picture heroes performing grave feats in dreary rooms with undressed women— happy crazy nose, tittly-lips, immense pride in the occasion of the night. Behind him stands my father, arm around me, his white fingers on my shoulder are obscured by the white wallpaper, he's glad, big vest, tight coat, all night he's been fevering and shouting in the party and "kidding the hell out of little Maggie ha ha ha"—now in the photo, coughing seriously, he's flushfaced, proud, holding me close so the world can see his love of his son in the newspaper, with the

same simplicity and believingness that Jimmy is holding
his joy-face up to the devourous worlds— My father is like
a Gogol hero of old Russia in a house. "Go ahead snap that
birdie there, we've all got our best smiles—come on Jacky,
smile, he never smiles that boy of mine dammit when he
was five years old I used to come home he'd be sitting by
himself on the porch one time he even tied ropes around
himself, gloomy little cuss, I'd say 'What you thinkin about
there sonny? What for you dont smile you worry your old
folks that have given life to you and dont know just how
to make up to you for what's at best a gloomy enough world
I admit—' "

"Hold still everybody!"

"Ahem!" my father clears his throat, enormously earnest— Flup, the picture's taken— I havent even smiled in
the picture, I look like a moronic boy with a strange pinched
(by sweat and camera shadows) drawn goofy peaky witless
face, my arms hang down joining my hands over my fly so
I look like an unnamably abnormal beast of a boy groping
dully his vain dreams of glory in a livingroom with big
parties around—looking like Pimple Tom of the swill piles,
sadfaced, droopy, but everybody sentimentally arranged
around me to protect the "LETTER ATHLETE HONORED"
as the picture caption says.

Suddenly in the other photo ("Thank God!" I thought
seeing it the next day in the Lowell *Evening Leader*) I'm a
Greek athlete hero with curly black locks, ivory white face,
definite clear gray newspaper eyes, noble youth neck, powerful hands locked separate like regardant lions on the hopeless lap—instead of having Maggie in my grip for the photo
like laughing happy financees we sit across the table from
little presents disposed thereon (radio, baseball glove, ties)—

still I dont crack a smile, have a grave vain look inwardly musing on the camera to show that I have special honors reserved for me in the echoey hall and dark corridor of this infinity, this telepathic bleak, this mig, instead of bursting into big laughs like Iddyboy is doing in the back stand-up row arms around Martha Alberge and Louise Giroux—going "HEE!" in a thundering boom cry and gloat of huge Iddyboy lifeloving girlhugging fencecrashing hungry satisfaction that has the photographer's hair leap up. Maggie, for her part, is a study of grave disrespect for the camera, wants nothing to do with it (like me) but has a stronger attitude, doubts while I pout, purses her lips while I stared wide-eyed at the world—for also my eyes grayly shine in the paper and show definite interest in the camera which at first is unnoticeable, like surprise— In Maggie there's disgust undisguised. She wears a crucifix and primly has no further word with world in camera.

30

The party ends, rides back home are arranged, taxis called—hoots across the snow, snowballs popping in the growl of spitting snow, cars racing motors to start, *vrroom*—no room. "Can we pile in back?"

"Nieh? I don knowa."

"Aint dee no room?"

"Beh sure! Come ah—"

"Bouee!"

Little teapots take their time.

"Good night Angelique—Good night—"

Calls across the snow—Moody Street a half-block down is a jostle of trucks beating chains, hoots, shovelers, the big blizzard has got men out working—"Hey I'm gonna get me some money," the old boys say down on Middlesex Street Lowell skid row and hop over on sore alcoholic feet to the City Hall or wherever to work for the City. Iddyboy mentioned it as the party broke up.

It has been a huge success—I had nothing to do with that part of it. The buses were running grace to God so most folks go home that way, Maggie who lives three miles away across all the city and out, has to take a cab— We get one down at Marie's all night stand across from where I live. I look up and see the dark windows of our tenement. Now that the party is over everything has the flavor of a dream well accomplished, like having a tooth pulled. Maggie: "This is one time you're not taking me to South Lowell and walking back to Pawtucketville."

"Why not?"

"Not even you could walk in this storm . . . ten inches of snow." Such Sicilian shifts my lamb of love:—I could walk in this storm as well as Colonel North Pole Blake of the Greenland Armadas and had done so to Pine Brook out in the Dracut woods, in the night, in big blizzards, carrying a long stick and planting it down so's not to step into streams entire, or well holes— I'd stood in the forests of night listening to the kissing of the flakes and the twigs of winter, the little sleet spitting like electric particles anticipatory and clicking, in wet gooey gum boughs—

"Yes I could walk in this storm—but I wont tonight, I havent got my overshoes except upstairs and boy am I sleepy wow—it's three o'clock in the morning!"

"Me too. Gee what a party."

"Did you like it?"

"Sure."

"How'd you like my father?"

"He was funny."

"Wasnt he? And we had a pretty good time. Gee some of the guys in there had a good time—"

"That aint the point," said Maggie pointedly.

"What?"

"It was in honor of you. You should appreciate it."

"I *do* appreciate it!"

"Nobody'll believe you if you talk like that."

"Well *you* understand. . . ."

"Yah," said Maggie, almost sneering, "that's because I'm just like you—" Moving her jaws in the history of our love, half tough-looking in the doorway, half-hunching over—I'm standing beside her proud, some of the boys in the Textile Lunch across the street can see I got a pip of a brunette waiting for a cab with me—I'm not old enough to chew my nails about not being able to go home with her and lay her. I'm chumpily looking at the upstairs windows of other tenements across the way, Maggie is primping her hair in her little mirror; a sad red ball light hangs in the ceiling of the Taxi tenement porch. Desolate shufflers come up Moody swallowed in the windy fall, athwarted by blazing flakes across the arc streetlamp glow. I kiss Maggie—she throws herself right up to me, loose, little, young, all I have to do is mention the word kissing and she'll play kissing games. I was beginning to sense her sexuality now and it was too late.

Across the street came part of our party, Textile Lunch

for hamburgers and coffee, they piled in, you saw a flash
of the jukebox, the counterman tattooed forearms on the
counter crazy-faced yelling "*Oy la gagne des beaux matoux!*"
(Oy the gang of ga-dam tomcats!) at Pa and the older friends
half drunkenly jawing into the steamy vapors of the diner,
wet, tired, not hungry, gloomily surveying and sneering
at everything—but exploding into laughs, big necessary
hassel jovialities and shows of neighing concern and sudden
good feeling tender and glad—The counterman makes a
slight slur in the corner of his mouth when turning to cook
the order.

Across, through vapor windows and fly snow, they could
have seen Maggie and me, up, side by side, in a doorway,
standing bystanders suddenly turning into kissers and again
resuming bystanders for stamping taxiwaiting tendencies.

"Your party was all right, I believe they couldnt a give
you a better one—"

"Yeah—not the point—I mean—were you glad to see
me tonight?"

"I *had* to see you tonight—"

"I know that but just to see me ha ha just kiddin ya—
you'll be all right. After some sleep and you get home you'll
be fine—"

"Jacky!" She's thrown herself, arms firm around my neck,
loins into mine, but back arched as she leans back to throw
her richness vision into mine—"I want to go home to a
house to sleep with you and be married."

I drooped to think about it—I had no idea what I should
do—"Huh?" I pictured my mother saying Maggie was "too
impatient," others talking about it, the sweet future of it
with Maggie and I getting home late at night tired from

a party, and going up dark steps along rosy wallpaper to
the dim velvet darkness of the rooms upstairs where we take
off our coats of winter and put on pajamas and in between
in the middle of both garments the nudities of bouncing
bed. A bouncing baby boy with Christmas in his eyes. In
the crib, in the rose dark, he with little poof pout sleeps
his little thoughts away. You couldnt disturb him with
rattles of talk and angels with sabers drumming up the
brown moth-swarming vision of the Drape, soon enough
they'd part, ascendant swimming Heaven *blazing* universal
snow particles of the truth—Maggie's baby in the reality—
mine, my son, in the snowing world—my house of brown—
Maggie's river making muds more fragrant in the spring.

   She went home in the cab, it was driven by a friend of
mine whose face I'd seen in a thousand Fellaheen dusks of
this village in our dirtstreet boyhood, Ned, Fred, he was
a nice kid, he made some joke about something as they
rolled off sadly big red taillight vaporing exhaust in grim
winter conditions and flopped chains off into distance and
South Lowell, source of my arrow.

31

Little paradises take their time. Little parties end.
   My father was only beginning to raise hell in the diner,
I went in for some tail end to my day, but only yawn a few
times in the greenish light and scarfed three hamburgers
with ketchup and raw onions while everybody carried on
the music and the roar of a good old Saturday or Blizzard

night in New England, at dawn bottles were opened, shiftings of parties took place, on Gershom Avenue at gray six o'clock when only the old ghosts of Pawtucketville walk wending their white way in black veils to church, there was heard from inside the tenements deep a sudden shrieking high laugh from some old gal in some roundtable black iron range kitchen and windows rattling black little boy cant sleep in his pillow, will be bleary for the blizzard in the morning—Me too I'll go to sleep now and make that black angel in the pillow void open—the world is not void open— "Go ahead Jacky me boy," my father even said rolling down off some big laugh with Ned Layne the wrestler who was part owner of the lunchcart, "go to bed if that's what you wanta do, and all you been doing is yawning, too much excitement for the kiddos tonight"—and Ned Layne would die in the war—nobody'd wrestled in the right arena around there—my sister's friend, the little chum of my sister's girlhood who was going to marry him was barking up a wrong tree in the serious reality of the open world. The tree that was with root of these realities had already threaded knuckly fingers in the bleak.

"Okay Pa, I'm going to bed."

"Did you like your party?"

"*Oui.*"

"Good—Dont tell anybody if they ask ya that I had a coupla drinks at the house, I dont wanta be obliged to kid laws." Before coming home to supper every night my father used to have his two or three shots of whisky in the Club across the way, it was the great time when I could see him head from there to the barbershop straight across the street, the long spacious handling of the scene of this with him inside strawhat hung up in summers' nights as I'm racing along on sneakers where we lived two blocks down, I was two years younger, see him unbelievingly rich in the shop with a magazine and a white barber shroud and the man knee-ing to his work as he shaves. "Good night kiddo, and if you wanta marry Maggie you'll never pick a prettier girl, she's Irish as the day is long and a damn good little scout as far as I can see."

32

"It's a warm coat I have," says Bloodworth walking in the cold north red dusks of March in Massachusetts near the New Hampshire line, "but it's not a warm coat tonight," making a sour joke and sullen, and suddenly I realize he's a great old skeptic who's thought deeply on the weather and uses it in his speech or has such horrid findings swear with it. "Christ, pretty soon the thaw'll be out."

33

April came. It joined with March in forming mud in the woods, long flying streamers of flags pennoned from the circus flagpole Post-No-Bills advertisements of May. Summer'd reach into the corners of spring and mop em all dry— the essential cricket would crawl from his rock. My birthday party was over, I grew more fond of Maggie now as she grew less fond of me, or surer. The season had swung on some invisible pivot of its own.

Thing was—Maggie wanted me to be more firm and binding in my contractual marriages of mate and heart with her—she wanted me to stop acting like a schoolboy and get ready to be busy in the world, make headways for her and our brood, and breed. Spring rank suggested this in breezes of prim river that now I began to enjoy as the iced ruts in Maggie's Massachusetts Street began to uncongeal, crystal, crack, and swim—"Frick frack" would wave the goodlooking hoodlum on the corner of Aiken and Moody Street and still your May'd come. "Damfool" will be the lark saying on a branch and I know that juices and syrup sops would pulse come throbbing springtime—"Never know would ye the wood was damp on the bottom" would be saying the old champions out in pine fields. I'd walk all over Lowell aweing and ooing my measures to the brain. Doves too coo. The wind like harp'll blow blah blah over Lowell.

Now I'm going to find out how my love for Maggie fares. Not too well.

I had no "Maggie what shall I do?" to ask myself and like a schoolboy finally decided that to hell with her my Ritz crackers and peanut butter would disappear. I pouted like a big baby over the thought of losing my home and going off into unknown suicides of weddings and honeymoons—"Honey," Maggie says, "it's okay, just go on going to school I dont wanta stop you or interfere with your career, you know what to do better than I do. You know, maybe you wouldnt be so practical to live with." It's a warmish late March night; I'm through the blazing moon the March witches are racing their shrouds and brooms, whippets come

after, yapping across the bleak, the leaves dont fly they're
mashed underfoot, a seething wet beast is rolling its back
in the earth, you're about to realize King Baron of the sweet
mountains was not going to be coronated in this Kingdom
pine sap—I saw blue birds trembling on wet black boughs,
"flute!!"

Fluting spring was racing through the corridors and ritual
alleys of my sacred brain in holy life and making me wake
and resurge to the business of being and becoming a man.
I drew deep breaths, cut shortcut quicksteps over the loose
crunch cinders of the back-of-Textile dumpside river-view-
ing gravel drive—the tremendous views of Lowell from this
ball perch of night, the countless sad tragic waters down
there, over shapes of dead bushes and rat-inhabited wrecks
of Reos Chandlers Pee Pee Poo machines of long ago, and
the bad sand, stinking of sewage—this I could smell in
spring tonights coming back from Maggie, spring'd send
the stale fender with its sweet rot swills caked underneath
and I'd know—this would be mixed with sweet breath river's
voice Awing at me over the lake of the bend—From Lakeview
clear I could literally smell the pinecones getting ready for
dry gladsummers on the ground, the azaleas were ballooning
again Mrs. Faterty's garden, Rattigan's saloon next door
would only send suds and breezy foam smells in the coming
months—you couldnt mistake spring from the mop handles
ratata-ing on porches of ladies—"There's my Pa now,"
Maggie is saying soon, as she walks down from the corner
where the South Lowell stores and bars were and passed the
joint where Mr. Cassidy's downing his boilermakers before
going home to sleep. "So I said 'We'll reach in get six, kick
one, kick two, kick em right in the lead then we'll spot to

clear and shove the rest!'—'What?' he sez to me 'I cant understand all that in one sitting—' 'Well for krissakes' I said 'you're gettin paid same as I am aintcha? And I been railing around here for seventeen years aint I? So you expect me to stop here and explain that to you again. Just keep your mouth shut and your eyes open—you'll learn—' "
Maggie walks by hearing this speech and smiles, goes home to tell her mother—Dark laughter. Out comes a little kid on the porch, and the moon. Among the brown Fellaheen lights of life I'm hurrying, off the bus at the cemetery corner and right down through a railroad overpass and big scrabbly lamplit plaza of two roads converging roughly and across that the pitch into that black barrel of Massachusetts Street South Lowell Night which has trellises, clinging vines, curly locks.

Spring blows in my nose, in my airy brain—The call of the railroad train is howdah'd on the horizon. Bending her head to me—"So you really dont want to get mixed up with someone like me—You may think so now but I dont think . . . it'll . . . work . . . out. . . ." I couldnt believe her, just hung around to neck some more. Unbelievably grim my view of life and the cemetery, Maggie thinks I'm just a lost thought dope trying to remember what he was going to say. I have three separate things to attend to in the arrangement of my mind with the tumblers falling and falling into place and the safe door opening slowly so slowly it was a lifetime— besides seeing she wouldnt love me now, I spent my time haggling over whether I should go see her or not. She just sat around and didnt care.

These teeth I also threw into the balmy redolent wind. Hands in pockets I trudged to the ghost. In the same way

I'd trudge the streets of Chicago in the night a few years later. Same way you see slanters coming through a storm from or to work, war, whorehouse door—

Everything went on as usual in the city itself—except that it was always changing, like me—though the chagrin of the reddy dusk up on Paddy McGillicuddy's street in the Acre up on the hill was mighty the same every time—and something eternal brooded in the sad red chimneys of the mills, ah these heavenward Empire knobs of a great civilization in a valley. The Kingdom of Lowell was bounded and tended thereto, from the paisans of the caucus out in (Michikokus) Methu-*enn* (Methuen),—?$Z&&!!*!—on out.

"You dont love me," she'd say with my lips in her throat. Okay, I said nothing. I had a lot of sawdust to work on in my poor kewpie doll. Sometimes, like my little sister used to do, I'd pretend to be asleep when Maggie said mad things. I didnt know what to do.

34

One night—impossibly sad how came my shadow—seeking the balm and ruby of her arms, lips—we had a date, had arranged it on the telephone. For weeks I'd been finding it harder and harder to get dates, she had developed another crush—Roger Rousseau, who used to play shortstop for the Kimballs in the Lowell Twi League at the same time his own unbelievable father with paunch and glasses played third base beside him and stooped to delicately lift his grounders off the grass without having to squat—They lived

in the country, were probably rich barons of this Kingdom
Lowell with medieval wall guards in their apple orchard
stonewall—Ran a dairy—Bloodworth had, with his atten-
tiveness, closeness to me, smooth grace and warm sincere
elegance filled her March hare months—but now we had
to deal with the villains of May.

Roger R. was coming around more and more. Fewer times
she'd let me come and see him try to come in—there was
a swing in the loamous backyard, she and Roger sat in it,
I'd never—Her little sisters looked at me differently; her
mother looked more pained; the old man just went to work
and had no idea who I was. Bessy Jones was away more.
The baseball was coming in: I'd made a new friendship,
with Ole Larsen the pitcher, for the season, and because he
lived on Bessy's street in a wood window wall a pebble's
throw from her rickety washline and they'd in the green
pale slur of youngling grass exchange comments over the
Tom Sawyer unwhitewashed fence . . . "Gee Maggie's giving Jack a hard time—"

"Yeah?" Larsen was 6 foot 4, blond, had shown interest
in Maggie but in the long dark histories of her neighborhood
he'd always laughed at her and never ever took to be serious—
Something Maggie mourned, she liked him—He was like-
able—"Well let him concentrate on baseball with me,
we're gonna have a great team this year." He believed in
us—sincere respect for our friendship—"You gotta learn to
hit that curve—"

The first day of Lowell High School practice I ran with
Freddy O'Higgins in deep left as the coach Rusty Whitewood
belted out a fungo ball that Freddy wasnt gonna make but
I was going to show that I could catch it, to Ole who was

standing beside the coach telling him about me and chatting
in general, I was all unknown in baseball, I ran over the
soft new grass clods and slanted and got behind and beyond
O'Higgins in his own left field (from my center) and tapped
the ground till that ball from high heaven came slowing
down and hugening for the ground arc over my head—
I reached the backhand glove and got it running away from
the plate . . . I brought it down almost stumbling, tucking
it in my belly, O'Higgins was not sure what I had just done
behind him, I heard Larsen Whoop! at the fungo bat—
Beautiful catch, beautiful spring—but I kept missing those
curve balls at the plate. When Ole pitched batting practice
he made sure to see I'd get just high hard easy easies that
I could belt to left—curves had me flailing silent plop
tragedies, foot in the bucket—fast balls I turned into new
fast balls going the other way and pulled and soaring—
sometimes I'd hit 420-foot marks mentioned by everyone
and when we came to play in the fenced-in park I hit
homeruns regularly in over center-feld fence in batting practice but the real game, the serious pitch, the chewing
pitcher, the razzing catcher, the crafty ball spinning in—
"You're out!" the bat pulling my wrists out as I squat after
it benumbed.

Larsen and I were buddies—I made catches for him—we
were goin to defeat Maggie. "Give her nothin! Let her worry!
Let her call you up! Dont mind her—pay no attention—
you got ball to play, boy! She'll come around again!" Ole
gave me advice. We rushed out to Shedd Park after the
third bell in drowsy late April afternoons and clutched our
gloves and spikes; it was heartbreaking because it was so
close to South Lowell, I'd look over the trees above the

cinder track for L.H.S. outdoor track, beyond the last tennis
courts, in the grieving birch, the first roofs of Maggie's
neighborhood Lowell—Then at night, after supper, I'd come
along the river—well she got tired of all that. Finally the
night we had a date, she broke it herself and just wandered
off to talk to Roger R. in the bushes by the railroad bridge—
in the sexy sand—

It was too much for me, my heart broke.

35

"You're a sissy," I thought. "Here's the girl you love that
you saw in the chorus line of the Keith's Theater in 1927
or 28 when you were five or six and you fell in love with
her thighs, her dark eyes—the angel of tinsel God'd dropped
you from them wings—Maggie —hit on the skull, dont
let her give you that sass." But—"She's the only—"

"Pay no attention to it!" my father said leaving to work
out of town again in his death-diving night . . . in seven
years he'd be no more. . . . The sun would shine on his
nose no more— "You're too young for that stuff. Get other
interests in life!" We're standing waiting for the bus on
Moody Street, we've been to the show before he leaves town,
the Merrimack Square where as of yore the rainy Rin-tin-
tin darkness the Fu Manchu balconies the spats of actors
but now we'd seen the new crackling movie of the moment—
"It wasnt any too good," my father's saying with a complete
dedicated sneer. "They try to pass the thing off, you know—
Well aside from that, kiddo, dont repent so. You make

mistakes and break your spirit worryin about it. You're the only one worried! Oh I know *cette maudite vie ennuyante est impossible*" (this ga-dam boring life is impossible). "I know it! What can we do? Just say, I'll be thinking all the time there's nothing but darkness and death, but I'd bet I've got to be busy with the wife and kids— All right—they cant make any better rafts than that!" He squeezed my arm, I saw the sad curl of his lips, the frank serious blue eyes in the big red face, the bigman grin about to asthmatically wheeze him coughing into a big laugh, and a bending down—For in the end Ti Jean was abandoned to his doom— and I stood and realized it. "I can do nothing in this—Say, now that track is over are you gonna make baseball your main sport? Well—I won't be here to see it, dammit. Ah," A brokendown sigh, "something was damn well supposed to happen that damn well didnt—"

"Where?"

Another sigh: "I dont know. . . . Maybe I thought we'd be closer this year—I dont know. Not only shows—trips, talks—we didnt do much—never do—Ah dammit son it's a terrible thing not being able to help you but you do understand dont you God's left us all alone in our own skins to fare better or worse—hah? So—you say where."—Another sigh. "I dont know."—"*Pauvre* Ti Jean, we got troubles eh?" Shake of head on around and back.

36

I was sitting on the slope of that park in back of G.J.'s house, an evening in May, 6:30, not yet dark, still light for some time, Scotcho is with us pitching little pebbles— at petals of May— My love, my sick sense, of Maggie Cassidy had grown into a tumultuous continuous sorrow in my noisy head. The dreams, fantasie varagies, wild drownings of the mind, as in real life I continued to go to school, hot spring mornings now outdoors, practically summer and no more school and I graduate from Lowell High.

In the winter track meets at Boston Garden in the Seaboard Relays I'd run a mad race against Jimmy Spindros of Lowell and others running for St. John Prep, wherever that was; *The Chief* they called Spindros, whose great hawk nose had made him stand in bleak fogs of old football games helmet under arm as captain of the Lowell team—long, tall, strong Greek champion of them all who died in the huge glooms of Iwo Jima. On the cork track of Boston Garden I in my little nail spikes took off with the same luck-jump off the imminent gun bang and flew around the banked turn in my own white lane as fast as I'd ever run in any 30-yard dash and got inside them (the three college runners) on the turn-in lane, probably illegal, behind me I heard them streaking right in my neck but I am flying and hold myself ready to bank into the far turn and wail right around on those nails throwing popcorks at the generation and coming off the board turn to hand my stick to Mickey Maguire who well cognizant of my love affair with Maggie had gone out and eaten big talkative hamburgers with Kazarakis and me in

the big Boston night, we all talked of our current girls and
problems and endured the harsh neons of that city in 1939
enjoying Greek out-of-the-way lunchcarts near North Sta-
tion where huge meatloaves were served to us as sandwiches
between bread, we'd eat contests— I've never run so fast in
all my life, Kazarakis is going to get the stick last and run
the gun lap, the final lap—as soon as Joe Melis bullnecked
huge battling the runners, with his football hips on banked
turns would—whoo!—come roaring in—Kazarakis was
going to really grab the stick from his hand, and elongate
his long waist for a sudden play of long legs and though
not tall 5:9 streak away thin and small but powerful and
somehow big and wham after the first turn with his stick,
groove into it, whir the great legs underneath his motionless
waist, you didnt see his arms, overtake and fly forward of
college sprinters—we won—but not because I finished my
lap ahead of Spindros of St. Johns, he came around the last
turn momentum-ing into his man and passed Indian Chief
Warrior bounding strides past me and handed the stick to
his own second man—I fumbled and broke up in the stretch
lost between the stick and the run— Mickey Maguire had
to sail off and pound and fly his way around the mad track
with a good eight-yard loss of lead—Kaz, the three of them
made it up— Some kind of defeat in that kind of Maggie
Cassidy must have brought me down— I'd reached my peak
of love and fabulous success for a night or two—when? One
night by the radiator in March she'd started huffing and
puffing against me unmistakably, it was my turn to be a
man—and I didnt know what to do, no idea in my dull
crowded-up-with-worlds brain that she wanted me that
night; no knowledge of what that is.

Her arms tight around me, her lips biting and foaming in the ocean of my face, her loins harping against mine in a big song of passion, love, joy, the winds of madness had with March run riot through her right through me we were ready for the fecund join with spring—and be man and wife in the Universal reality—I even already pictured my little red window house by the railroad tracks—for us—in muddy walks under brown lamps down Massachusetts Street on soft spring night, when I know all the guys of Lowell are running after trucks of excitement, the chicks are making riddles from a hay-rack with pendant breasts, the whole American night's a-ranked around the horizon.

I'm sitting in the grass of the park with G.J., I'm dreaming straight ahead of me.

Life is sweet, inside of a big cave.

"I'm goin over to see Maggie." I tell Gus—looking under the big trees out at Lowell over the field across Riverside Street—over its waving weeds we could see two miles away rooftops of Christian Hill shining red in the sun, the Kingdom was more beautiful than ever, my Baghdad Fellaheen rooftops up and down little Pawtucketville were creaming into rose for me— I was the beloved youth—blade of grass in my mouth, lying in the slope after supper, seeing— letting the winds of evenin ripple hugely in the trees above, at home, *patria*, land of birth. No idea some day our Kingdom would be overrun by vaster Kingdoms invisible like superhiways through the dump.

"Dont bother with her Zagg," G.J. is saying, "I wouldnt lose myself over no broad, let em all go jump in the lake— my ambition in life is to find some way to achieve *peace*. I am I suppose an old Greek philosopher or something Zagg

but I'm serious when I say, screw it— Maggie's been doin
nothin but playing you woods, if everything you tell me
is true—she's done nothin but give you griefs you big babe
greek—all of us know it, Lousy, him and Pauline told me,
I was hurrying back from Lowell Commercial College and
there they were on the corner of Central and Merrimack
with Pauline just went in and bought a new dress in Kresge's
across the street up there and I was supposed to help them
but anyhow—help them with—I say, fooey on it!"

Leaning over to palm up his hand earnestly, on an elbow—
Lousy's spittin silently over an evening blade which doesnt
even budge as he zeets one—but lifts waving boles as he
zeets through his teeth softly, like a man whittling a stick
at nightfall, a man closing his snap knife on a wood barrel
and you hear it across the breeze at nightfall— I thought
G.J. was all wrong, I knew better than he did. I said to
myself "Well G.J. doesnt know—we—my family—what
I'm like—he cant judge even though she's been so mean
and me passing up Pauline Cole just to be—he doesnt know
what he's talking about fuggen G.J." My Ma and Pa'd often
told me not to hang around with G.J. For some reason they
were afraid of him, *"Yé mauva"* (he's vicious).

"What you mean he's vicious?— He's just like us in the
gang—he's all right—"

"Non. We know all about him and his vices—he talks
about it all the time on the corner—Papa heard about it—
what he done with little girls—"

"He doesnt have any little girls!"

"He does *too!* He says he's got a fourteen-year-old girl—
He goes around making dirty speech like that, why do you
bother with him!"

"G.J. doesnt understand that about me," I reflected, "my—everything I have to put up with and learn and see—and Maggie loves me."

I looked into the soft sky and the moon was coming out pale and cradled in the earthly blue, and I was convinced that Maggie loved me.

"Dont believe me then," says Mouse. "They'll deal you every kind of pitch they can think of Zagg to get a penny out of you—dont worry I know women I saw everything in my own house with relatives plus in-laws and big fights among Greeks of standing in this community of Lowell—you don't know the half of it, Zagg." Spitting—not like Lousy for eve calms, but for expression, sproosh. "They can take their lousy ga-dam mills down there on that dirty old river dump and stick right up their ass for what I care, Zagg—I'm leaving this Lowell," jerking his thumb at it, "maybe *you're* not but I am"—looking at me seething with rage, retribution in his popping eyes—G.J. was growing up his own way.

"Okay Mouse."

"Where you goin now?"

"To Maggie's."

He just waved his hand. "Get in her pants for me, Zagg."

I laugh through my nose and started off. I saw G.J. move his palmed hand—blessing good-by—okay.

I roamed off, negotiated whole Lowells walking down the main arterial mainline vein of Lowell, Moody Street now Textile Avenue, sweeping down on clacking shoes to go find my gory-dowry. "G.J.'s wrong as day."

Night night. Impatient to wait for the bus, I hit Kearney Square on foot a minute ahead of it and jump into the South

Lowell bus for roaring wailing rides with the great driver
dumping all his passengers most of em in the last streets
now just has to bang through out of town tar construction
trolley torn-up sewage under outlying streets and blast along
just missing holes, posts, fences, to the car barns outside
town now turned slick redecorated garage—eying his watch,
timetable, his wild interests in time coinciding with mine
as I leap off the bus at Massachusetts Street just underpass
and be sent skittering on little feet as he continues his
roaring journey, goes up the road blinking big red lights—
The void of the universe surrounds the lonesome walker—
I negotiate along the banks of the Concord, actually just
walking in the middle of the street and seeing it through
little bungalows, back orchards, abrupt little river down
to the little shore, nothing big about the Concord but full
of acorns—

Maggie's not down at the end of the street with her dress
flapping and us singing *Deep Purple* as in the lonesome
romance of winter when we'd melted together under frozen
stars—now molten faced stars of easy summer were blearing
on our cold love—no more bad cars passing us on good
roads—"Jacky," she'd said, "————," untranslatable
love words best to keep secret if you can remember em at
all—

"But now she aint standing in no road," I'm telling
myself, hurrying up, the light that made G.J. and I see as
we talked about her now faded in the west where she was
hidden—

"I think she went down through that broken fence, Jack,
down that lane—the kids are swimming or talking about
swimming tonight." This is Maggie's kid sister, smiling

bashfully at me; in a year they'd be saying she had crushes
on me, others, but right now still a little girl and writhing
around a post to play hopple dee skotch with Jamie ma
mop, appata pippity pappety poo—

37

After that it was just a question of getting on with the
ambitions that my family and I had decided for my life so,
I went to New York with my mother and we saw Rolfe
Firney at Columbia who'd written after my old high school
football coach Tam Keating had touted or scouted me to
his old friend of the Boston dog races Lu Libble, Lu Libble
the big Columbia coach, both of them in the "ribbon com-
mittees" of the great crazy dog racing night of electrified
rabbits in the huge darknesses near Suffolk Downs with its
giant gas tank so huge that I keep seeing it by dog tracks
and by the sea in my life— I was going to make my pipe-
smoking golden-windowed dormitory studies in this great
university of the world. I was so proud that when Boston
College and Coach Francis Fahey later of Notre Dame tried
to get me the following summer I didnt change my mind
but stuck to my idea of New York, Columbia, Horace Mann
prep school, despite the fact that my poor father wanted me
to go to Boston College because it would secure his recent
new job in Lowell in a printing plant that did all the jobwork
for Boston College, Emil Duluoz once more popular and
solid—nevertheless both my Ma and I had minds set on
Columbia— The additional details were that of a "football
talent search," another story—

Rolfe Firney received us politely, showed us the athletic offices where the faces of the gentlemen seemed to me immensely and richly and beautifully important, men with white hair, grave, grand, all well-dressed, opulent, courteous. I proudly brought my mother to see all this before she returned to Lowell. She'd traveled to New York to arrange for my room and board with her stepmother in Brooklyn where I was going to live while attending Horace Mann prep thereby riding the subway every morning from Booklyn-of-the-red-heart all the way to Broadway and 242nd Street a total insane twenty miles—I liked it though, because people are interesting in the subway when you're seventeen and you've never savored the big city. I was a really contented kid to see myself at last among the great mountains of glittering buildings. Horace Mann School was built in ivied Tom Brown gray granite on top of a cliff of solid rock—behind it was a beautiful athletic field of green grass—a gym with vines—You saw the immortal clouds of the Bronx floating in the Indian sky and dont tell me it isn't an Indian sky. Below the cliff toward Yonkers lay the vast Van Cortlandt Park for the beautiful decathlon athletes stretching their white aristocratic legs in fields of shrubbery and foliage Jews and Italians of a new heroism of another sort of Kingdom Lowell.

Superstitious of midnight the first night we slept at grandmother's in Brooklyn I lay awake for hours listening for the creak of the ghosts of New York in the house, hearing faintly sounds on the Brooklyn street like lovers late in summer city night giggling in each other's necks by the moon of shipping; it was an altogether different Lowell, and so all opening-out into the big megaphone hole of the world from those Rudy Vallee lips of Merrimack Square and Maine that

I knew that it was getting lost like a marble ball rolling
down eternity in a bowling alley opening out to darkness
down to infinity rockets cells telepathic shock tape.

I lay in bed thinking I was going to be a big hero of New
York with rosy features and white teeth—an idiomaniac
post-Iddyboy incarnation of the American Super Dream
Winner, Go Getter, Wheel,—and white snowy scarf and
big topcoat with corsaged girls in tow and no teetotaller I
but big journalistic champion of off Times Square (like The
Little Theater) as I had seen newspaper tragedists in B movies
talking over beers in stale barrooms of neon winking Manhattan night hatbrims lowered like Marc Brandel or Clellon
Holmes heroes brown taverns thru the pane glass written
Bar & Grille you see the blackracked giant Neon Sign of
the Owner of The Paper—Cigar Mouth Mann, grandson
of Horace, hardhittin tough jesuitical editor, mainline artist,
phlegm screamer of silver blary screens of the Rialto all the
times that winter between Maggie and High School I'd
played hooky in but now I'm in New York viewing the real
thing from a scared bed in Brooklyn, seventeen. Gulp.
"G.B. Mannpram, Pub. of the Manhattan Manner Post
Evening Star," planes are flying in with serum, and I'm
sitting in the bar heroically brooding over the way I just
smashed the waterfront gang and G.B.'ll give me a raise
(I see G.J. raising his leg to burp, "All right J.D., the job
is yours, b-r-up, and dont cut me out of any of that offshore
oil of yours"—) and I head for my penthouse, bored with
the loose overcoats, shroudy hatbrims of big alcoholic newspaper new york and change casually into evening clothes
(dinner jacket with velvet lapel glossy like London fires in
a grate, which shine on it making vellum pools of rich wine-

bottomless substance on my wealthy breast), and say hello to my wife, idly—

Through her balcony window you can see New York skyline in the starry night lace-dim behind sheer curtains, the sherry and the cocktails are ready, we can hear a piano tinkling from the Gershwins upstairs, and our fire crackles.

Oh how our fire crackles—how lovely the swan of her throat—I lie bedded in black night sending up white puffs of dialogue balloon for my gold encarvened dreams— Dear Angel Gabriel broods over me, listening. (Logs from old Adirondack in the penthouse, my hunting gun is there, early Jack London rich Frisco heroes of the penthouse have invaded New York via Lowell Mass. the viaduct from landing beaches and cold pines of the St. Lawrence River, over the *mer* the Breton fisher boys are snarling up the nets with salt cracked hand and have to do it all over again—) My whirls of world-seeing race around the room, I gulp to see vast mothers of light swarming around, and to hear my brother tree in no more wilderness outside in Brooklyn scratch a fence in a little Brooklyn August breeze. My dream has in it a wife beautiful beyond belief, not Maggie, some gorgeous new blonde gold sexpot of starry perfection with lovely lace neck, soft long skin, inturned mouth top—I pictured the gorgeous Gene Tierney—and the voice that went with it, Kitty Kallen, Helen O'Connell, a young beautiful American girl getting excited in your arms—

Next day, in any case and aside from the validity of these dreams, my mother and I strolled arm in arm across the grass of the Horace Mann field—bleachers, goalposts, the English Gothic roofs, the headmaster's own rose-covered cottage made of stone—a Kingdom military fort overlooking other worlds—already at seventeen I'd formed the idea to some day draw maps and write the history of another world in another geography of another Africa, another planet of Africas, Spains, pains, shores, swords—I had little knowledge of the world I lived in.

It was a rich school for young Jews ranging from age of eight all the way to sixteen, eight forms in all, you could see them arriving now at the school in limousines with their parents to give it the once over. It was high, warm, beautiful. "O Ti Jean how nice it'll be in this little paradise! Oh boy! *Now* it's making sense!" my mother said decisively. "Now we've got something to be proud of—you're going to be a real little man in this place, it's not just old regular schoolteachers or one of those dirty old places your father went to in Providence one time and always talked about it and now he wants you to do like him—*non*, go here, and go to Columbia, that's the best idee." In her head my mother saw herself living in New York walking in the big lights of the great exciting world and the great shows, rivers, seas, restaurants, Jack Dempsey, Ziegfeld Follies, Ludwig Baumanns in Brooklyn and the great stores of Fifth Avenue in New York— Already, in my little childhood, she'd brought me to New York to see the subways, Coney Island, the Roxy—I'd at age five slept in the tragic subway of buried people shaking from side to side in the black air of the night.

I had a scholarship at Horace Mann, paying most of my tuition; the rest was up to me, my father, my mother; I helped get a lot of publicity for the school in the newspapers in the fall—there were 10, 12 other guys like myself— "ringers" from high schools everywhere—bruisers, we murdered everybody except Blair (0–6), it was a scandal—the bruisers, they too'd had their loves, tempestuousnesses and sadnesses of sixteen.

"Now you're all set," said my mother as we walked among the beautiful clean halls, "we're gonna buy you a nice new coat to look nice in this little place that's so *cute*!" My mother was positive in her secret heart that I was to become a big executive of insurance companies. Just like when I made my First Confession, I was a little angel of pure future.

38

She went back, everybody exchanged huge letters—To prepare myself I fixed my room at my grandmother's with dusty old books from the cellar— I seriously sat in the flagstone yard of little flowers and woodfence sometimes with a drink like ginger ale and read *Lust for Life* the life of Van Gogh I'd found in a bin and watched the great buildings of Brooklyn in the afternoon: the sweetish smell of soot and other smells like steam of a great coffee urn beneath the pavements—sitting in the swing—at night the buildings shining—the far train of great howls on the profound horizon—fear grabbing me—and with good reason.

I started football practice but sometimes played hooky to see shows all alone on Times Square, drank huge milkshakes for 5¢ impossibly aerated like cotton you drank illusion of liquid like the taste of New York— I took long walks in Harlem with hands clasped behind my back, staring at everything with great interest in roaring September dusks,

no idea of the fearful complexities that would arise later in
my mind about "Harlem" and blackskinned people— I got
letters from G.J., Scot, Lousy and the Vinny—G.J. writing:

All fooling aside though Zagg, I just cant seem to get used to the
idea of you being away. Sometimes I come out of Parent's Market
and say "Well I guess I'll go to Jack's and listen to the 920 Club,"
then I remember you're away. In one way, I'm glad you're in New
York though Zagg, because down here it's worse than the Sahara
Desert. By that I mean it's dead. Same old thing day in and day
out. It's monotony at its highest. I'm going to school as a P.G. this
year Zagg, or at least if I dont change my mind I'm going. My Ma
promised me she would try her hardest to send me to college if I
did. The way things are now it's a very faint possibility, but I'm
hoping for the best. That's about all Jack except don't forget to give
your Mother my best regards. [He thought she was still in New
York with me.] And here's hoping you have the best of luck in
everything.
                                   Your Pal
                                   GUS

Scotty in his brown house kitchen sat down at his mother's
round table by the stove and wrote: "Hi Zagguth ye babe:
Well I'm—"and talked about his work—"so when I go on
days again or better still—"and then talked about Lousy in
a way that made me see it had rained on a lot of things
since Maggie'd spurned me in sweet Lowell, a bleary new
barrel was filling, and all would drown in it—

By the way Lousy left Machinist and is now looking for a job as a
foundry man. He's wacky. He ought to stick to Machinist but Zagg
did you ever see a guy so bashful to ask for a job. This morning I
learned that the Diamond Tool needed a man for a telephone job.
I went and got Lousy and when we got down to see the boss you

know big office Lousy wanted to turn back, because he was afraid the job was to be nights *when he didnt even know*, Zagg, so I had to make believe I needed a job and Kid Sam followed me in then we filled out the same old application and Belgium never let out a word. I'm telling you Jack he's got to talk his way into a job and if he acts this way he'll be a goner. I'll have to bang it into his head. Well I'll hear from you yet Jack and, you also from me so I'll say good night now as it is approaching the second hour of the Thursday and in about 15 hours I get $29.92 for my last weeks' pleasure. Your pay, SCOTTY, Write Soon.

Iddyboy, from Connecticut where he'd gone to work: 'He thee boy!''—
Vinny wrote like he talked straight from the scene—

He tried it everyway he could, after we got through with her she still wanted more, Zagg please believe me I never seen a woman so hot in all of my life, a female rabbit and you know her very well. B.G. is her initials and she lives next door to me I dont want to write her last name down on paper but you know who I mean. Lousy and Scot were gone to show the unlucky stiffs. Well that's all in a lifetime I guess. Albert Lauzon still goes to the Social Club at half past 4 in the afternoon so he can be sure to be there when the joint opens up good old Belgium —[Lousy'd started to shoot pool in earnest in green night]. Well you old screwball I guess that's all for this time answer soon. Hope that you get lots of tail during the time you will be out there my saying is "there's nothing like a very good fresh piece to refreshen yourself."

VINNY
Turn Over
Other side

P.S. (A HORRIBLE UNPRINTABLE P.S.—
SIGNED SHASSPERE)

Have pity on the next girl you take on.

39

I went through the football season with a bang, there were
big explosions of fiesta on the fields of folly and autumnal
golden screaming glory—and the 7th of November all of
a sudden when I was established and already vexed, mixed,
blest, guffawing in the immense things of my new life, new
gangs, new New Year's Eves—when on little envelopes for
memo I'd write "Keresky job" or "Garden City Defense"
(study of the opposing team's diagram) or "$5 Lab fee" or
"write math formulas in subway"—and had about fifty crazy
screaming friends who climbed the steep hill from the subway to the palace of the school in the red mornings always
haunted by new birds—voila—bang—comes a letter from
Maggie, and on the back of the envelope (in words as dreamy
as an old touchdown before dead men) it says: "Maggie
Cassidy, 41 Massachusetts Street, Lowell Mass."

Jack,
    Right off I am going to tell you who it is, it's Maggie. Just in
case you want to tear this letter up.
    It must seem funny to you, to have me writing to you. But that's
beside the point. I am writing to find out how you are and how you
like school. What is the name of the place anyhow.
    Jack wont you try to forgive me for all I have done to you. I
suppose you are laughing at me *but I am serious* really.
    About 2 weeks ago I met your mother and sister downtown. I
just spoke I would have stopped and talked if we had been going
together at the time, but I felt ashamed, if they had even asked me
if I wrote to you I wouldnt know what to say.
    Jack cant we make up I am so terrible sorry for all I have done.

I dont know how it is but some of the fellows you know have been trying to date me up as soon as they found out we broke up such as Chet Rave and some I would much rather not mentioning. I like Chet but not to go out with. He told me your address after much teasing. Bloodworth has been askin for you also.

Well Jack so long if you dont answer I will know you dont forgive me.

MAGGIE

In the study class, thinking, but also seeing the funny face of Hunk Guidry our center on the team, I passed him the note to read, to show him I had girls, he said no. He wrote on the envelope: "Some shit! You're a heartbreaker just a Casanova."

I wrote to Maggie a little later.

40

I invited her to the spring prom. After a few preliminary letters, and I'd learned all about the way things went with their big program of dances.

In November I went home, hitch hiking with my madcap friends Ray Olmsted and John Miller; John Miller, Jonathan actually, a horn-rimmed genius-knobbed hero of the New York Central Park West thickcarpet, his sister played piano, at dinner his lawyer father'd say *"Mens sana in corpore sano—"* "A healthy mind in a healthy body"—which was one of my proudest sayings about myself and coming from an aged lawyer— Ray Olmsted was the tall good-looking Tyrone Pemberbroke of American Love Magazines, hand-

some, a flat hat, a pipe— They didnt get along with each
other, they were separate friends of mine; we had lost adventures on an old New England road, hasseled through
New Haven, proceeded to Worcester—dark roads of early
hitch hiking with a turkey dinner at the end of the string.

Night. From wild subsequent events with mixups of my
gang of Lowell and the New York smart boys such as Lousy
breaking a huge windowpane on Moody Street from nothing
but sheer glee that Olmsted and Jonathan Miller were so
mad—in other words I had brought the gang the cream of
the wild Horace Mann world then, looking briskly, I'd
dodged out and cut down to see Maggie at an appointed-
by-phone time and she hit me from the side with kisses as
I half turned away from too much the moment I saw her
and we started bending back big kisses to the carpet floor
and lurching and pushing in big climax kisses of movie
magazines' photos—the seriousness, the long Latin study
over lips, the furtive over-the-shoulder peeking at the paranoiac world— But Maggie had tears, and wept her little
dimple chin under my bent neck me with my hair hanging
low like a French beast now looking into his wild Parisian
woman for the lifetime of love—we're about to learn the
great lay of life pun blunt. But we dont have time, it's an
exciting night when everything's happening not only to you
but to everyone because of to you!—we're glowing, rich,
sick to happiness, I look at her with such love, she with
hers, I didnt see any prettier lovers in the sunflower prairies
of Kansas when larks squawk in thrashing sunset trees and
the old hobo hoes out his sad old can a beans from the pack
and bends to eat them cold.

We loved each other.

Therefore no immortal love blood was exchanged between us that night, we understood each other with tearful eyes. I would see her Christmas—soft sweet time.

41

I ran home from school and arrived the 21st of December— many things behind, many in front of me. In church I gazed at the old rosary beads of my First Communion given to my by my Aunt Anna of Maine— The golden crucifix now darkened but terribly beautiful the little tortured image, the fists, the little muscles—*Inri* inscribed always like the mark of the mute—the feet nailed on little blocks of yellow metal in my hand—I looked up high, the roof of the church, it's an afternoon service, a great big high school church service, gray dark Sainte Jeanne d'Arc basement, former Mayor Archambault is attending and the priest will mention him— Next to me, front, sits a beautiful honey-colored girl, Diane de Castignac of Pawtucketville, I dream of forcing her to some kind of anteroom to wrestle and moan with her, back of the altar, she has nothing on underneath, I force myself on her and finally surprise her by really getting her and completing the job—charming, juicy— When the church service is over I'll file out with everyone else and there she'll be by the door in the aisle, I'll brush my lips on the sleeve of her coat, she'll say "You'd better!" (we've already made an appointment for later)— Out on the church porch instead of going down the steps in the Lowell real rainy alley gloom I go over the balcony, bump Ernie Malo's

head with my foot, he says "Ouch" and oldlady-crazy guy
kitchen houses in back, scuppers, board fences, garbage
gangs of Brooklyn, I climb and come somehow to the tremendous sea, iron purples brood on its fantastic scape, clean,
clear, I rush down the sand, the waves of dawn are enormous,
our boat is to the right waiting, I'm going two years before
the mast to that desolated spectral North Pole— The purple
clouds, the gigantic waves—I jump in and dash around
scared—the cannons are booming over the surf—Morning
and new seas.

"But dont nettle the rose," said the beautiful Visage of
the Virgin Mary as I stared at it.

As though She'd never come to me, but could only come
to women and men of final Last Quartets of life not raw
me's. But I pray. For the success of all my things.

I'd already been to the redbrick hotels of midtown New
York in 1939 and had my first sex with a red-headed older
girl a professional whore— I'd gone around boasting about
it like all the other maniacs in the school, had gulped in
the bed waiting, she came down the hall on sharp heelclacks,
I waited with a pounding heart, the door opened, this
perfectly built Hollywood beauty piled in with her wealth
of heavy breasts—I was terrified— I'd even told Maggie
about it but not directly, hinting at it in letters in some
way that she caught on— She was just as awed as I was.

So I'm in church worrying about sins, syphilis, girl of
my heart and dreams—home from school—neat combed,
big coated, I nod politely as Mme. Chavert nods politely
at me, I'm getting to be a big grown-up man of Lowell . . .
with histories of events in New York, awed news, futures—
enemies imaginary and none otherwise—

New Year's Eve Maggie wants me to do to her what I
did to "them girls in New York"—

"Aw Maggie I cant do that to you!" I say, thinking it
too sinful bigcity to do it to her and not realizing my arms
are broken on a dumb idea. But Maggie is frightened too,
she "shouldnt a said it!" she thinks—we're on the porch,
in the wintry cold of Jan. 1, 1940— I have also been
drummed with the idea that if I want to marry Maggie it's
better to wait.

At home I tell my mother that I love her and want to
marry her; time to go back to New York is near, no more
walks to Maggie's three miles down the cold sidewalk—I'll
have to go back to my books, friends, huge Metropolitan
interests in everybody— It makes me cry.

"Okay Ti Jean—I know you love her— You've got to
finish school to fix and prepare yourself for your times—
She'll help you if she loves you—if not, she doesnt love you.
You see that? Your studies will count in the end—by that
time she'll realize everything. Tell her what I said—I'm not
interfering in your affairs. You dont have to tell her if you
dont wanta— But take it easy— Dont hurry, girls nowadays
invent all kinds of troubles— Little Maggie seems okay—
go—go see her, tell her good-by—Try to arrange for her
to come like you say to your little dance in New York. . . ."

My father was gone by then.

I saw Maggie, said good-by, we looked tearfully at each
other and she with new woman eyes deeper than and showing
through her own eyes amazing me and making me feel on
some wheel of nature.

42

Everything is perfect; I get invitation cards. They are big cards with gold paint, and RSVPs chrome tipped like the Chrysler Building. I send one to Maggie.

At the last minute, she wrote me: "Jack, Well I guess I'm in for a swell time Friday or should I say this week end. Call me up at my aunt's before you come over so I will be sure to be ready. And by the way I am wearing a pink gown with blue assesories. You know what if you can get me a wrist corsage get it if not it's O K" (no signature).

Ah, terribly sad the look of her writing on envelopes. In the dust of my black books I saw the moons of death. "Wow," I told myself, "is it true I want a woman?—" I felt sick, "Ruin all my—"

43

From sweet Lowell Maggie came to sour New York in a rosy gown.

Corpse ridden Hudson rounded about the Glitter Isle of dark New York America as we raced to the April Prom in a taxi cab across Central Park. The preparations, events, all enormous— She'd come with her mother, stayed with her aunt, was staying the night of the Prom at Jonathan Miller's family's rich apartment, arrangements I had made in earlier attempts to save as much money as possible and probably suggested by Jonathan in the first place as in his brief profound friendship with me he directed my affairs and influenced my mind.

Now we raced across town in a cab—I was all dressed in white tie and tails. During that winter the uncle of Gene Mackstoll a London Man About Town Sam Friedman: "Here you are, Jack"—giving me the suit from his closet as nephew Gene grins "you ought to wear it for the Spring Prom. Take it. It's yours. Here." He gave me other things— To make myself handsome for the Prom I'd got a sunlamp sun tan in the Hotel Pennsylvania with a shave for about two dollars, like a Cary Grant I wanted to walk into the barbership clacking on heels head stiff courteous and cosmopolitan and have myself led to a chair saying something tremendously witty—or and with a feeling of rich security—instead it was a lonely walk among empty mirrors along the backs of empty barber chairs with an at-attention towel-wristed barber waiting at each one and I chose none in particular and was pulled up by no Ricardo Riduardo to my authority chair. The lamp burned and gave me a terrible lobster red face for the ball.

Maggie has put on the best thing she has—a pink gown. A little rose in her hair—the perfection of her moonlight magic Irish sorcery suddenly seeming out of place in Manhattan, like Ireland in the Atlantis World— Trees of her Massachusetts Street home I saw in her eyes. All week just because G.J. had jokingly written "My hand still burning from having been sat on by the perfectly rounded buttocks of M.C."—this made her so valuable I wanted her to sit on the hand of my hope—I held her tight; felt suddenly protective in this big cab crossing the glittering Manhattans.

"Well, Maggie," addressing her through all her troubles getting down from Lowell and everything ready, "there it is—New York." Beside us, Jonathan, himself bemused on the skyscrapers with those seventeen-year-old intellectual first thoughts weighing him in and everything to me inconceivably glamorous because of his addition to the scene—

"Humpt—t'aint much to *be* in—looks nice," says Maggie—her lips curled— I bend down to kiss and hold back, feeling myself too importantly dealing with Maggie's proper reception tonight to be just kissing—the two of us miles apart in social fear, minds wandering to other matters like the ease of pain in the breast that wants out—not as in our sweet river's nights—not as in love—but to little paranoiac wonderments in the complications of gowns, evening clothes, the corsage I had to rush and get—tickets, furlibues—to make you sigh—in brief, we were doomed to an unsuccessful night, I would never know altogether why.

Her little shoulders had freckles, I kissed every one of them—when I could. But my face was burnt from the lamp and I kept wincing and sweating so I worried what Maggie thought of me. She was too busy being snobbed by the wealthy lavishly gowned girls in there who'd not struggled 250 miles from a railroad brakeman's old house by the tracks in day coaches of the railroad with the necessary striven-for free pass the gown in a box—but had had checks for half a thousand dollars waved under their noses by indulgent millionaire fathers who'd said "Go down to Lord & Taylors or someplace and get yourself something real nice impress the boy invited you—" For their shoulder blemishes and freckles they had sorceries of powder, boxes of shield-soft, sweet nascent poofs of puffs to dab all over and the best stuff available—Maggie didnt even know it was done or how to do it or how to know. Snowily they swam around her like swans, her tawny shoulders with touch of pink from last summer's sunburn and freckles of Ireland were bedazzled by priceless necklaces and earrings. Their snowy arms were advantaged and powdered and glittered; her life arms were hung.

I sneaked her down to a little bar downstairs, in the basement of the Hampshire House, Jonathan was with us, for a moment we were like gay people in an Irene Dunne comedy took over a lounge and no one's around and Jonathan officiated to make drinks and we giggled and talked and I thought we were in some wood panel New York of carpeted luxuries and Maggie felt better being alone and snuggled up to me—

Jonathan (in tails, behind bar) "All right, Jack, if it's not Tom Collins I shall have to expel you from our haunt, all I can make is an exorcization dont ask for more—" I look proudly at Maggie for her to see these big words. She's looking around skeptically. Her gardenia hangs sadly. My face is on fire, stiffly in whitetie collar I'd bent to a hundred conversations upstairs feeling that as I inclined my nose politely to the speaker's nose it would reflect red on his face a big flush of silly heat—

"Oh fer krissakes Jonathan get it over with!" Maggie's yelling as John tried to joke and goofed— Finally we were discovered by others, the parties floated in, we went upstairs again. A dazzling affair. A horde of young generation in white tie with promflower girls attending a melee, a gathering, in a building, a tower—crowded—rousing applause, speeches, music inside. Greed oozing from the Oos and Aas of false hellos and dreary compliments and presumptive conceited good-bys. Dancing, talking, looking out the window at Central Park and the lights of New York—all of it horrible—we were lost—our hands clutched but with empty hopes—just fear—empty chagrin—longfaced party in real life.

44

"Jack let's get out of here, let's go away—" She wanted to go to secret bars, ballrooms, be alone— I thought of Nick's in the Village— But the arrangements had been made for a gay party of cars to go downtown, uptown, places— She sat in a corner sofa, against me, almost crying—"Oh I hate it here—Jacky let's go back home and sit on the porch— I loved you much better with your skates—your earmuff hat—anything but this—You look awful—watsamatter with your face?—I look awful—everything's awful—I knew I shouldnt of come—I guessed it— Something was wrong— My mother wanted me to. She persuaded me. She likes you, Jack. She says I dont appreciate a good boy when I see one— The hell with it— Give me home any time. Jacky," taking my chin and turning my face to her, looking swimmingly, littly into my eyes with her small perfect eyes here lost in the hurrahs, white roars, chandeliers, "if you want to marry me ever dont ever try to have me come to this New York— I couldnt stand it—There's something about it I don't like— Oh let's get outa here— The hell with all these people—"

"They're my friends!"

"Friends?—Pah—" She gave me a scornful look, as

though she never saw me before, and surreptitious—"Bun-cha no good loafers— Some day'll be begging at their back-doors and they wont even give you a crust of bread you know that as well as I do—Friends—for now friends—later it's good-by Jack— You'll be on your own, you'll see— They wont throw shirts at ye when it starts raining in the mountains. And isnt she the huffy puffy one in her dress cut low enough to show her breasts to the lot of us the hussy she must have more sass than my sister Sissy and seventeen others—"

"You're all s's," I said.

"All s's and dont give a shit. There! I wanta leave. Come on. Take me to a burlesque. Take me anywhere."

"But we're supposed to go to the cars after—lots of plans made up by a whole bunch—"

"I like that Knowles playing the piano—he's about the only one I like—and Olmsted—and Hennessy I guess be-cause he's Irish and you dont catch *him* here do you? Humph: I've had my see, my fill of your famous New York. You know what you can do with it. You'll know where to find me from now on, Bub. Home. Good old home . . ." Dizzy, sweet, all the combined ankles of your raving beauties couldnt measure against the atom of Maggie's flesh in the crook of her underarm, all their eyes, diamonds and vices no competition on the keen point of Maggie's Stardust Per-sonal Me.

"I'm not even looking at *any* of these other women—"

"Aw go on—there's that Betty everybody's been telling you about all night— Why dont you go dance with her— She *is* beautiful— You'll make out in New York—crap's paradise—"

"What are you mad——?"

"Oh shut up—— Oh Jacky come home have Christmases with me—never mind all this charivary—fancy fanfares for nothing—— I'll have a rosary in my hand at least—to remind you—— Little snowflakes'll fall on our pretty roof. Why do you want these French windows? What are the towers of Manhattan to you that needs love in my arm every night from work—— Can I make you happier with powder on my chest? Do you need a thousand movie shows? Sixteen million people to ride the bus with, hit the stop—I shoulda never let you go away from home——" Rich lips brooded in my deaf ear. "The fog'll fall all over you, Jacky, you'll wait in fields—— You'll let me die—you wont come save me—— I dont even know where your grave is—remember what you were like, where your house, what your life—you'll die without knowing what happened to my face—my love— my youth—— You'll burn yourself out like a moth jumping in a locomotive boiler looking for light—Jacky—and you'll be dead—and sink—and you'll be dead—and lose yourself from yourself—and forget—and sink—and me too—and what is all this then?"

"I don't know——"

"Then come back to our porch of the river the night time the trees and you love stars—— I hear the bus on the corner— where you're getting off—no more, boy, no more—— I saw, had visions and idees of you handsome my husband walking across the top of the America with your lantern—shadow— I heard you whistle—songs—you'd always sing coming down Massachusetts—you thought I didnt hear, or I was dumb—— You dont understand the dirt—on the ground. Jacky. Lowell Jacky Duluoz. Come on home leave here."

She saw aces of spades in my eyes; in hers I saw them glitter and shine. "Because I'll never come to this New York to live you'll have to take me at home and as I yam . . . You'll get all lost around here, I can just see you— You shoulda never left home to come here I dont care about anybody says about success and careers—it wont do you no good— You can see it with your own eyes— And lookit her with her fine and fancy ways, I bet she's as balmy as the day is long and they have to spend thousands a dollars on bug doctors for her—you can have em brother—so long. —Huh," she concluded, through her throat, which throbbed, and I kissed her and wanted to devour her every ounce of her mysterious flesh every part hump rill hole heart that with my fingers I'd never even yet known, the hungry preciousness of her, the one never to be repeated altar of her legs, belly, heart, dark hair, she unknowing of this, unblessed, graceless, dull-eyed beautiful. "They can put me away any time, I'm ready," said Maggie, "but dont let the birds sing in *this* hole—"

Out of her eyes I saw smoldering *I'd like to rip this damn dress off and never see it again!*

Later my sister said "Did Maggie wear her hair off the face?—or in bangs?— She has a small face— Did she wear rose? That would go good, she's so dark." She wore bangs— my little bangs of Merrimack.

45

Somewhere in the vast jewelry of the Long Island night we walked, in wind and rain— Sunday night—the week end over—the drives, cocktail parties, shows, scheduled arrangements, all fulfilled, without fun—her gown long packed back in the box— She pouted as I conducted her sheepishly across those unknown darknesses of the city— Her aunt's house was somewhere across an empty lot, down a street— The gloom of Sunday night—the wind blew her sweet hair against my lips; when I tried to kiss her she turned away, I groped for the lost kiss that would never come back— In the house the aunt had prepared a big Sunday dinner for us and for Mrs. Cassidy who'd sat out the week end and humbly—helping in the kitchen—a trip to Radio City.

"Did I hear Jack say his belly was empty. You feel weak?— come on, here's soup—"

"Well kids did you have fun?"

Maggie: "No!"

"Maggie! aint you got better manners than that."

I helped her off with her coat; she had a cotton dress underneath; her sweet shape made me want to cry.

"Maggie *never* liked Boston or any place," Mrs. Cassidy told me, "pay no attention to her, she's a devil— She likes to wear her old sweaters and shoes and sit in her swing— like me—"

"Me too Mrs. Cassidy—if I didnt have to play football—"

"Come eat!"

A huge roast beef, potatoes, mashed turnips, gravy—the kind Irish lady plying me with double helpings—

After dinner heartbrokenly I sat across the parlor from Maggie and watched her, half sleepy, as they talked—like home, dinners, drowsy in the parlor, the sweet legs of Maggie— Her dark eyes scanned me contemptuously— She'd said her piece—Mrs. Cassidy saw we werent getting along— The big expedition, plans, the big prom, flowers,— all down the drain.

They went back home on Monday morning after a night's sleep, Maggie to her porch, her kid sisters, her swains coming a-visiting down the road, her river, her night—I to my whirlpools of new litter and glitter—standing in the corridor of the school Milton Bloch who later became a songwriter introducing me to Lionel Smart ("Nutso Smart" to the math professor) who later became my great sweet friend of the modern jazz generation, London, New York, the world—"This is Jack Duluoz, he thinks Muggsy Spanier has the greatest band," and Lionel blushing, laughing, "Count, man, Count"—1940—rush to the Savoy, talks on the sidewalks of the American Night with bassplayers and droopy tenormen with huge indifferent eyelids (Lester Young); school paper articles, Glenn Miller at the Paramount, new shoes, graduation day I lie in the grass reading Walt Whitman and my first Hemingway novel and over the campus field I hear their rousing applause and valedictories (I had no white pants)—

Spring in New York, the first smell of woodsmoke on Third Avenue on the first unfrozen night—parks, loves, walks with girls, styles, excitements—New York on the

lyrical perfect shelf of America in the Night, the Apple on
the Rock, the green blur of Coogan's Bluff over the Polo
Grounds firstweek May and Johnny Mize of the St. Louis
Cardinals poles a new homerun—Bill Keresky's sister
Mickey in black silk slacks in a penthouse, her red lips and
rings of sixteen under eyes, soft initial on her breast—Duke
records— Wild drives to the Yale campus, around and
around Mount Vernon at midnight with hamburgers and
girls— Frank Sinatra incredibly glamorous in loose hanging
suit singing with Harry James *On a Little Street in Singapore*
not only teenage girls digging him but teenage boys who'd
heard that sad Artie Shaw clarinet in California on the quiet
perfect street in Utrillo— The World's Fair, sad trombones
from the shell, over the swans—Pavilions with international
flags— Happy Russia— Invasion of France, the great Pow!
overseas—French professors under trees— Mad Marty
Churchill reaches into subway and knocks man's hat on
floor as train pulls out Har Har Har!—we race on El plat-
form— Waking up one Sunday morning in David Knowles'
Park Avenue apartment I open up the venetian blinds, see
young husband in homburg and spats conducting beautiful
dressed wife with baby in carriage through rippling golden
suns, beautiful not sad—A *crème de menthe* at the Plaza,
vichyssoise, paté, candlelight, gorgeous necks—Sunday afternoon in Carnegie Hall.

> Spring dusk
>   on Fifth Avenue,
> —a bird

Midnight talks over Brooklyn Bridge, freighters arriving
from Montevideo— Wild generations jumping in a jazz

joint, hornrimmed geniuses getting drunk on brews— Columbia University ahead— Borrowers of binoculars in Mike Hennessy's bedroom looking at the Barnard girls across the green—

Maggie lost.

46

It was three years later, a cold snowing night, the Lowell Depot was crowded with late arrivers from Boston clutching *Daily Records*, rushing to cars, buses. Across the street the depot diner did a thriving business, hamburgers sizzled juicily on the grille, when the counterman with his old Montana face let go a batter of pancake mix on the dull gleaming fat of the grille it shot up a sizzlecloud, loud, as doors squeaked over and the boys off the train came in to eat. The passenger train, the 6:05 or 6:06 had just left, a freight was rumbling through Lowell in the winter dusk snow a hundred cars long, its tail-end caboose was riding after at the Concord River Bridge in South Lowell near Massachusetts Street—the locomotive was nosing through lumberyards and wholesale plumbers and gastanks of Lowell downtown back of the mills and Chelmsford Street, out in the yards on Princeton Boulevard the rolling stock was still in the dribbling snow sweeps. Down Middlesex Street and over the tracks, a few dull gray battered doorways hid a few Lowell waiters in the storm. The Blagden restaurant wasnt doing much business, brown on a corner, a few dull eaters inside, a cafeteria lunchroom. In back, the Blagden Garage and Parking was almost all done for the evening rush. The garageman had just wheeled back a big truck into place, against the partition wall, and squeezed the last Buick against the fleet deep in the far end of the garage, there was not much space left. The garageman was alone, walking back with his car keys, pencil and tickets, thick thighs hurrying—in a half dance. At the big overhead door he whistled to see the storm dropping softly in the alley; above, a gray tenement kitchen window glowed dully—the garageman could hear kids talking. He turned into the small potbelly office with the rolltop desk, threw the ticket tab on the desk among papers and cigarette packs and threw himself in the swivel chair and turned it around and shot his feet to the desk. He reached down and slugged out of a quart of beer. He burped. He picked up the phone.

Dialed. "Hey there, is that you Maggie?"

"Yeah. Jack? Calling agin? I thought you was all through with me—didnt believe it—"

"Yeah! Come on! I'll come pick you up right now—We'll drink beer in the office, play the radio, dance—I'll take you home—a big Buick—"

"What time?"

"Right now!"

"You sound like you changed."

"Sure. Three years makes a difference!"

"Last time I saw you—was after the Prom—you remember—college boy—"

"I aint no college boy now.—I'm goin in the Navy next month."

"You *was* in!"

"Just merchant marine—"

"Well you were better off—But I'll come—"

"Same old Maggie," thought the garageman, Jack Duluoz, calculating, "I'll be over in twenty minutes sharp. Be ready. I've got to bring that Buick right back. This is like stealing a car. And I'm leaving the lot unattended—"

"Okay. I'm ready now."

"Okay baby," said J.D. "see ya" hanging up and leaping to his feet. He took out keys, went out, locked the door of the office, tried it—walked over to the overhead door just to give it a yank, slapped it, strode back deep into the garage to the Buick, and got in.

The car door frumped softly. It clicked open again as he leaped out and put out a few garage lights— In the gloom now he foraged sadly after something. Then slowly the motor started, he backed around, shifting, came front, headlights flashing—lighting up the shadows of the garage— The horn tooted as accidentally he moved his elbow convulsively in search of cigarettes—Looking suspiciously over his shoulder he drove around, through the door, out into the snowy alley— He wore no hat, just a jacket— Only a few months before he'd been a reporter on the Lowell newspaper, he wore the wild look of a man emancipated into the redbrick heap of night from some bank jail and so gleaming and furtive he looked around frantically with a wild head everywhere hearing imaginary noises and seeing traffics and checking to make sure to be ready—incredibly slowly the Buick crawled to the mouth of the alley. The snow thickened. *"Jack o diamonds,"* sang Jack, *"Jack o diamonds, you'll be my downfall,"* pronouncing it "Jack o doymonds" as in his memory of G.J. Rigopoulos thus singing it New Year's Eve night of 1939 when he'd first met Maggie this girl he

her in this Buick late tongith in the garage, deep— "Baby," he
said out loud, "I'm sure gonna get you tonight—aint gonna be
like it used to be with you—I'm gonna find out about you at
last— I've had women since you, and traveled, and been
far—the stories I could tell you'd make your little Massachusetts Street sit pale in *this* star—about railroads, and
bottles I throwed, and women brought me gin for supper, and
old bo's I followed across fields to hear them sing the blues—
and moons over Virginia—and birds in the same place in the
dry morning—rails leading south, west—dusty places I sat
down in—slept in— Things I've known in the morning at
office desk, school desk, personal bedroom desk—Romances I
had on gravel—on newspapers in parks—on couches of beery
fraternities— Dances I've known alone at night windows—
Books I've read, new philosophies I've made— Thorstein
Veblen, my dear—Sherwood Anderson, sweet—and some
man they call Dostoevsky—and North Pole mountains I've
climbed—So dont manage me off tonight, I'll slap your wrist,
I'll drive you inta rivers, I'll show ya—" As he talked he drew
out of the garage driveway into Middlesix Street having waited
for three cars to pass and now barely ahead of three others he
swung to the right, on over the tracks, looking fearfully into
the hole of night each way for engines of the crack, past the
depot, diner, Merrimack Hotel—where, he knew, Reno the
owner of the Buick was just simply with his woman in a bed
and wouldnt come out till morning and if tonight at all much
later—At the foot of the steep hill of School Street at
Middlesex he swung up with courage trusting he needed no
chains in the mad new snowfall—

Traffics flashed around. He ground up the hill, stopping at the rotary momentarily to see, swinging right, giving leeway in the glorietta hobbyhorses to cars from downtown Lowell, swinging around all the way and on down School, driving confidently now, picking up speed, interested in the dangers of real life confronting. Down past the Commodore Ballroom, down past Keith's Academy, and with the black great Common white and blacktraceries on the left on down toward South Lowell and Maggie's house.

47

But it hadnt changed. Sadly the garageman gazed at the warm lights of the house, the rutted road, the dull streetlamps, the dead vines on winter's porch, the shape dear and loving and half hauntingly unclear of some old couch-form against the corner of the porch where so long ago he'd swooned the wine of the moon in other youths and when his youth was young—

Maggie, at the toot of his horn, ran out. He couldn't see her face. She came around to the door of the car. "Dont you wanta come in see my folks?"

"Nah nah come on—"

She came in, frightened, climbed into the machine on her hands and knees as with the difficult leg-up she tried to throw herself in to sit. "Well there you are—you dont look the same—"

"Why not?" he demanded.

"You look thinner but you're not a kid any more—you're a kid but you look . . . cold hearted er sumpin . . ."

"*Cold* hearted!! Hah!"

"Er sumpin— How about me did I change any?"

He started the car, looking swiftly. "Sure—you're the kind of girl'll always look the same—good—"

"You didnt even look."

He was pushing the car down Massachusetts Street desperately for something to do dodging mudholes black in the snow.

"Yes I did."

They thrashed and fought deep in the Buick deep in the garage at two o'clock in the morning, the sweetness of the girl was hidden from the boy by a thick rubber girdle at which he pulled and yanked, desperately drunk, poised at the gate.

She laughed in his face, he slammed door shut, put out lights, drove her home, drove the car back skittering crazily in the slush, sick, cursing.

FOR THE BEST IN PAPERBACKS, LOOK FOR THE

In every corner of the world, on every subject under the sun, Penguin represents quality and variety—the very best in publishing today.

For complete information about books available from Penguin—including Puffins, Penguin Classics, and Arkana—and how to order them, write to us at the appropriate address below. Please note that for copyright reasons the selection of books varies from country to country.

In the United Kingdom: Please write to *Dept. JC, Penguin Books Ltd, FREEPOST, West Drayton, Middlesex UB7 0BR.*

If you have any difficulty in obtaining a title, please send your order with the correct money, plus ten percent for postage and packaging, to *P.O. Box No. 11, West Drayton, Middlesex UB7 0BR*

In the United States: Please write to *Consumer Sales, Penguin USA, P.O. Box 999, Dept. 17109, Bergenfield, New Jersey 07621-0120.* VISA and MasterCard holders call 1-800-253-6476 to order all Penguin titles

In Canada: Please write to *Penguin Books Canada Ltd, 10 Alcorn Avenue, Suite 300, Toronto, Ontario M4V 3B2*

In Australia: Please write to *Penguin Books Australia Ltd, P.O. Box 257, Ringwood, Victoria 3134*

In New Zealand: Please write to *Penguin Books (NZ) Ltd, Private Bag 102902, North Shore Mail Centre, Auckland 10*

In India: Please write to *Penguin Books India Pvt Ltd, 706 Eros Apartments, 56 Nehru Place, New Delhi 110 019*

In the Netherlands: Please write to *Penguin Books Netherlands bv, Postbus 3507, NL-1001 AH Amsterdam*

In Germany: Please write to *Penguin Books Deutschland GmbH, Metzlerstrasse 26, 60594 Frankfurt am Main*

In Spain: Please write to *Penguin Books S.A., Bravo Murillo 19, 1° B, 28015 Madrid*

In Italy: Please write to *Penguin Italia s.r.l., Via Felice Casati 20, I-20124 Milano*

In France: Please write to *Penguin France S.A., 17 rue Lejeune, F–31000 Toulouse*

In Japan: Please write to *Penguin Books Japan, Ishikiribashi Building, 2–5–4, Suido, Bunkyo-ku, Tokyo 112*

In Greece: Please write to *Penguin Hellas Ltd, Dimocritou 3, GR–106 71 Athens*

In South Africa: Please write to *Longman Penguin Southern Africa (Pty) Ltd, Private Bag X08, Bertsham 2013*

FOR THE BEST IN PAPERBACKS, LOOK FOR THE 🐧

FOR THE BEST IN PAPERBACKS, LOOK FOR THE 🐧

Plus:

THE PORTABLE BEAT READER
Edited by Ann Charters

Includes excerpts from Kerouac's major novels, poems by Allen Ginsberg (including *Howl* and *Kaddish*), extracts from William Burroughs's *Junky* and Neal Cassady's *The First Third*; and selections from the work of Herbert Huncke, Gregory Corso, Gary Snyder, Lawrence Ferlinghetti, Michael McClure, Diane DiPrima, Anne Waldman, Bob Dylan, and others.

688 pages   *ISBN: 0-14-015102-8*

OFF THE ROAD
Carolyn Cassady

Carolyn Cassady vividly and perceptively brings to life her two decades in the heart of the Beat movement and her involvement with many of its leading figures, including her husband, Neal Cassady, Jack Kerouac, Allen Ginsberg, and others. This fascinating memoir reveals another side of the life and times Kerouac immortalized in his classic *On the Road*.

448 pages   *ISBN: 0-14-015390-X*